Reductio ad absurdum

Read randomly for is that not the way of life
Flick to a page, beginning or end
If not sated just flick again
Strange mutterings from someone's mind
Question or criticize as you please
Open or close it as you choose
Your eyes shall guide the way
Ignore it and leave it unopened though a question mark remains.
To what depth does this penman reach?
Is there purpose to his script?
Other than his own search for the essence of validity
that lays hidden in his soul
The penman the scribe
reaches out to you
from the emptiness of a once blank page
now blotted with selfish visions
that life be more than just shadows
You are my redeemer
Bringing life to my imaginations
My philosophical ramblings

Reductio ad absurdum
Paul Charles The Unconventional Scribbler

The Unconventional Scribbler
Presents
Walking on the wrong side of Harmony

ISBN

Freedom for Awareness Publications 2018

Dedication

My Granddaughter Cora
Born June 29th, 2018.
To her mother, my Daughter Charlotte.
To her Aunty, my Daughter Amy

There are no words, for the love, pride and gratitude
that I feel,

Preface

This book came about, simply through 65 years of life experience and emotions
In truth all began in sorrow and continued throughout the years. There is another whole book that could be written about my life. Who knows I may attempt to write it. However, the pieces contained within, are simply observations, emotions and I hopefully sometimes inspiring.

We each in our own ways must go through life facing difficult issues, many of which we may bury mentally, in the hope they remain buried.
Sadly, that is rare, for there are always triggers waiting to open unwanted memories. However, if we could find the freedom, or be given the freedom to have access to our greater inner selves, if perhaps the young were shown the beauty of the natural world. If the earthly human powers that be--- taught the essence of compassion, rather than indoctrination, into that of; greed, segregation, and war mongering. Just perhaps our species may come about to. live with less suffering.

How this book came about; I write, I have no idea what I am writing, or where the words come from. I glance at the finished article and think yeah I understand that, I will share it.
I do not class myself as a poet because I do not follow structures.
So, there you have it.
How should the book be read.? Turned by page, flicked, rummaged, random selection, the choice is yours, I have an image of someone with a red pen crossing out mistakes, adding punctuation and changing grammar. Hey that is fine by me. Doodles are great also.
The hopeful outcome for me, the author, is that, if one word, can help innovate, motivate, or lead to awareness in whatever manner. Then it was all worthwhile.

The Unconventional Scribbler

Introduction

Regardless of, who I am
I remain independent of; Everything.
My opinions belong to me.
I write/talk and create from mine own experience.
I am a **Philoet**, not, poet.
A creative expressionist, not, an Artist.
A hopeful motivator of thought, not, an influencer.
Lastly, I turn to nature, not humans,
for guidance of my life.
My main interest**.**
FREEDOM for AWARENESS.
And
The Individual right to exist.

Harmony, balance and well-being

The Unconventional Scribbler

Contents

An opinion only

(*The Unconventional Scribbler*)

There are many labels ever creating greater confusion
as to an individual's conception of their state of health.
The powers that be and advanced technology have taken away freedom of thought.
Religions have turned people from natural compassion and acceptance.
medical sciences have over populated the world with drugs
and everyone is a therapist.
The young have very little conception of time.
And schools have lost their structure and purpose.
Politics has become a farce that no longer serves the people
And the media has no bearing in the world of reality.
We the ordinary peoples of all nations, countries and cultures
Have been indoctrinated into false perceptions,
We are robbed daily of our human rights.
Daily we are led, further into the realm of consumerism.
Mental health issues have become an epidemic that affect us from birth
Due to greed, ignorance and politically correct agendas.
Freedom has long passed us by, stolen from all the above.
Sadly, it shall continue to be so, until finally the powers that be
bring about, destruction.
As the bible says, beware false prophets. How true especially against itself
Maybe it is time to be rid of that which has no proof nor bearing
And return to the natural world of reality and wisdom.
Perhaps it is time to accept the truth of our slavery to political and religious dogmas.
Perhaps it is time for the standing of; individual humanism and the right not only to be alive
but free from the tyrannical invasion of privacy that surrounds us now.

A Woeful tune

Life can be rough…that's tough
it needs be dealt with
for past has passed…. get over it
Acceptance is now, what else to fear.

You are but human…what makes you so special
For lack of nurture.
There is that of sorrow
Not enough love.
To much time…Wrong era.
Wrong environment, oh woe.
For each positive you find a negative
watching energy and freedom pass you by.
Such woeful remorse.

Yet what if, not that of woe
but Wow, oh wow, I live
am equal in all of life
to live in that of harmony
to discover that of true balance, grateful for breath
I live, I live, never woeful again shall be.

Acceptance

Reaching into the depths of one's soul.
that, which is called, mine, Me, I,
How though can It be known if?
this is all a part of the same source, or, of other.

Yet what of this other, that which appears separate in so many ways.
This outer something, connected and yet independent of;
the essence of being, divine presence, angel of the unknowing self.
The true self of understanding, meaning and wisdom.
That which protects us from madness,
from the insanity that haunts our awakened state.

How though can one not believe?
when nature herself, has shown the many wonders of; unexplained magic.
How can there be no purpose, how can there not be,
that which is, other than.
This 'other than' which has been recognized throughout the years
has been noted in many languages
under many names
in many shapes and form,
how can no truth be attached?
Am I soul that lives in a body?
Is, this soul governed by, spirit that is even further outside of the self?
I am of no earthly master, yet, am of spiritual guidance.
Where then within the laws of time stand the truth.
What seed brings forth life in its endless forms.
No words seem to suffice, and yet,
the aching, the passion and desire of connection, stream through my physical body.
The scream inside me has no voice, just a vibration of longing passion.
I formulate my words to a divine essence, unto that which I feel,
yet have no knowledge of, in name, nor gender, or, form.
Therefore, divine essence of all being.
I ask only, that you ever guide me, along the path of;
harmony, balance and awareness.

Age is of no consequence

Age is of no consequence
nor gender or creed.
For each of us from birth
all carry that seed.
The seed of addiction
hidden deep in the soul,
waiting for that moment,
we lose our control
It has no preference of; kith or kin
when those destructive behaviours
broil, so deep within

It has no care for job or home,
as it leads you blindly
to a life alone.
and once we have experienced
our addictive choice,
then gone our identity and own true voice.
With no higher spirit
there is nowhere to turn
as destructive behaviours
and self-pity, we learn.
With no higher soul
the addiction shall win
With no higher self
the pain grows within
There is no blame
just self-choice of life
to live filled with love
or die full of strife.

All in words

All in words
Words of promise, of failure
Of loves conquest and loves doom.
Words in a jumble of languages
Words of compassion, words of war
Words that are selfish words that are misused
To many words devouring mind space.
Words of no effect, words of instruction, of indoctrination
and worthless destruction.
How can this be, is this what was meant when the creation was created
NO not with words
Words that clutter, that clutter, that clutter, burying the soul
Defeating the spirit
De-valuing life
Where is the meaning, of what construction, what importance?
To they who starve
And of the child, deserted and alone
What words will give that child
nurture and shelter
What words can give back that which has been taken
What words will make the poor rich
The sick will not be healed, or addicts cleansed with only a word
What language has but the words of nature?

Life is more obvious when not distracted by words.
what words that you
now read will alter the course of history,
or open the heavens to shower us with wisdom.
Is wisdom within words, or is the wisdom in using words wisely
How easy it is to control and incite
What prophet could have turned the heads of many, without words
Lies are words, as are promises
Are words truly the gift of life
Could we be, without words?
All these words just to arrive at simplicity of life
Actions are far greater than words
Life is but a short passing phase why waste it with words
when we can fill each moment with, pure action of doing.

All that is

I awoke, and I thought of YOU
I asked myself, do I really care
I looked out in to the morning sky
And realized you are everywhere.
I have no name by which to call you.
No idea of your nature, gender nor form.
Just that you exist somewhere and are worthy
Within this creation of which we are born
I look back through my years of existence
I question my follies and woe
I reach out to the coming of my future
But it is only in the now I can grow.
I awoke, and I thought of YOU
And I realized that to be alive is to care
So, for today I open my heart to life
And appreciate ALL that is everywhere.

All that we capture

The wonder of imagination
The experience of life's terms
and all that one learns
The pleasures of nature
Enthrallment of rapture
in all that we capture
inside of us burns

The knowing of growing
The purpose of knowing
The cause and the reason
no matter the season
The moments the feeling
With all we are dealing
the before and there after
is all so revealing

Why hide from the presence?
The extreme of the essence
The life of the heartbeat, ever incomplete.
Neither in balance nor in harmony
yet seeking synchronicity, within the shadows of; our own deceit.

An open book

When physical love has abandoned you
and darkness veils your path.
Seek beyond the stars,
where your true soul awaits your call.
For love awaits you in the forests,
as beneath the ocean's waves.
upon each beam sent by the sun
to spread in harmony.
All of this is within your palm
reach out, release, let go
breathe in the pureness of nature's breath
amid the golden glades.
Tis here sweet soul in timeless time
that our auras shall become rainbows
a guiding path for others.

The book lays open before us
words reaching into soul
a wall painting hangs invitingly
offering fantasies to enthrall.
how each heart has longed this pure essence
that offers such creative choice
for within this journey of new freedom
shall a soulmates voice be heard
whether through telepathy or upon the astral
the spirits shall guide our course
and the journey of our entwined oneness
love and harmony shall endorse.

And what of Eden

What talk of love shall bring forth wisdom
What open hand shall capture another's heart?
What loneliness upon they who seek the void
What purpose when facing death.

Tis not misery that I now speak of
Nor is it pain nor suffering nor ill will
Nay this is natural poison of man's load
A traveller within mists of time
Forlorn, often weary venturing far and wide
Testing inventing seeking discovery
To ease the aching soul.

We are but two, of this creation
Given gifts to aid our plight
Generation upon generation
Seed of Man, and woman's egg
Yet what lessons learnt
through this endless time

Our heritage of bloody wars
What lessons learned from they who starve….
…...such slaughter of tender lives
What purpose to, this life we live
What value to natures course.

All but we are in harmony
With the rod of purest wisdom
where once were gods to look down upon
Now in sorrow have turned their heads
From the destruction they see,
the pillage of man
Eden, no longer to be seen.
What point these words, of endless plight?
recall of echoed cries where so many wise have fallen beneath the feet of;
they with no essential soul

And therefore, all shall continue
This warring of humankind
therefore, it shall continue.
Sweet birth beholds thine death.

Another Day

Shadows of life, corners of time
the living of wonder
early morning awakening
the new turn of day
peace, hope, harmony.
Balance of the heart,
connection to all creatures.
Life in all its glory, the beauty of the land
the essence of natural being,
such wonders to understand
pureness within its own existence.
The very breath of originality.

Angels demise

They fell, haunted by the past
Caught in a net of despair
Separated, alone, frightened,
Broken and forlorn.
Wings shattered against the cliffs of time.
Raging hell stormed around them
The spell of paradise now broken
Such anguish and sorrow as the angels fell

All hope now passed
All dreams shattered
The glory of heaven at war.

Thousand upon thousand demons risen
Splintering from the ravines of hell
Time now far beyond gods scope
Faithless tears frozen in fear.
Cries of shame distorted
Rainbows of joy dissolved into darkness.
Such sweet angelic song crushed
as heart of man fills with sorrow.
Bound into darkest night.
Bellowing, raging, a storm of remorse,
Regret for ancient sins.
To late the trumpets blare
To late the fateful cry
For revenge, now released, to ravage
Risen to take its toll
Where once green meadows lay,
Now churned pits of unshared souls,
Clutching, grabbing,
Seeking solace,
Seeking peace,
Seeking self
Too late now the drums that beat
To late the redemption poll.
For hell have fury rent
Upon the turns of time.
What fear is this, what fury spent?
Unleashed upon such creation
All power now ceased within and without………………

Angels demise

…………. the sun hidden in the darkest shroud.
As the wings of hell grow stronger
Coveting all in sight

No righteous prayer now heard above
As warriors screech out revenge
No child's whimper of innocence
Ever to be heard again.

Spirits of greed and gluttony
Roar out their fiendish freedom
Whilst eyes of time watch with moistened eyes
Powerless to intervene.
Such howling winds scour the land
Leaving no stone unturned
Each life force now but prey to death,
To late the heart of reason.

Seas sucked dry, lands ablaze
Mountains scattered far
Such ravaging of a world once known
no longer the pulse of life

Such madness spread within us all
On the day of risen hell
The saddest day for all mankind

The angel's sad demise.

Animals

Strip away the desire,
the pride, the greed, the envy and jealousy.
The high demands because of another's word
Who can know the answer?
However, through thought and unreasonable argument
There soon can become a weakening within the being, the soul, spirit, and true essence of self.
Whatever that may be.

So many words, contradictions and hypocrisy, the cry for God.
Goddesses of old, the elements and images.
To angels and those long dead
Woeful the lament and questions sought
The falsity of being, lies and deceptions
Presumptions, failings and false perceptions
How can it be known of these things?
How can belief, separate ignorance and wisdom
when our species continue to create,
un-balance within the world of which we live?
Can this be failings, what failings are these.
How can there be, failing, compared to what, to whom?

Tis true I repeat myself.
Over and over, I ramble from my own being and its life experience
Perhaps I believe myself to be unique
Perhaps no different to; the greater many.
It is sad that I not of your thought.
Whether you are protective, critical, enraged or contemplative
I question mine own judgements, as that of mine sanity also.
However, it is all never mind
You live within your conscience and I within mine
The only similarity between us is fight, flight, feed and fornicate
Animals that we are with are
Glorifying in our superficial intelligence,
and overpowering ignorance.

As One

In purity and innocence, we are born,
blessed with, the wonders of natural life.
The greatest gift that lies within us; the gift of; love.
A true gift, of our pure inheritance.
It is this pure love from, from which I speak.
having searched my soul, the essence of self
I communicate from the core of my heart,
for I have searched your soul also
Our journey shall be as one, together
blessed through the eternal spirit.
Together, through this union, may we know wisdom,
speak from our hearts, sharing all that comes before us,
May we know that of; harmony, acceptance, and peace.
I can but offer you, the pureness, and strength of my very being.
Therefore, before all that is and all, that has ever been
I ask this day to be blessed
and each day that follows, that we journey together
united in body, mind and soul
Ever respecting our individuality, as well as, our union,
along each path that we may choose to walk together, **As one**.

As you ever step

As you ever step forward into the next phase of your journey
how easy to believe that, fate is sealed?
That choice is out with your own ability.

What though if you were to question this, as a truth.
For there is but one truth, a reality,
with which we all are destined from birth
That which, brings about
demise, death; the passing over, into.
That unknown.

However, choice of living, the how, the where, the what for,
Is none other than, personal responsibility, throughout, allotted time.
As is, that of self-opinion and judgement upon others.

As with all choices
there come's many different directions,
all with a variation of outcomes.
Yet there is none who can evade, the last breath.
The last chapter, verse, sentence and characters within.
May it be that, each author writes with,
Wisdom, awareness and mindful compassion.

Awaken

As I awaken unto the day
more questions come my way
As I investigate the past
searching the life in which I am cast
I find more chaos than that of peace
With jumbled thoughts that never cease.

Never sure of right or wrong
Or the proper place that I belong.
a prisoner withheld in mine own mind
Where natural peace I cannot find.
Tis for this folly I find not fact nor reason
Of day, nor week, nor that of season.
Nor that of present with urgency,
or, my future, my legacy.

Tis though I await a saving grace
To find for me the perfect place
Where all desires become destiny
And my world becomes full of harmony.

Sadly, the fantasy is never true
For we are responsible in all we do
And the longer we remain shadowed in the past
Less chance to live the pure life cast.
Therefore, tis my desire, to live in now
Aware of all the why's and how
Then perhaps I may discover the truth of me
Creating a future that sets me free.

Awakening

Awakening the spirit within.
A precious moment,
that arrives,
silently through, the pathway of; self-awareness.

No easy task.
No simple decision.
No set patterns.
No choice of time, nor pre-set arrangement.
Just arrival.
Recognition.
acceptance of and the welcoming of.

For that which was, is of no more.
That which has become, is as rebirth.
Bringing with it, no knowledge of knowledge,
Nor of learning.
Nor of wisdom.

Awakening the spirit within
You become only that which is.
An essence of natural being.

Balance

Perfecting self, awakening soul
Growing with essence of life.
Living In awareness, gratitude of time
Alive in all that is.
Such wonders behold the being that seeks
The reflection within harmonies path.
Tis in this time that all be true
Equality of spirit and mind
No matter of name nor form envisaged
This gift belongs to all.

Barren land

Nature's perfumes in all surround
The perfect textures of growth and ground
Yet here was I, dead to Gaia's voice
Alone in bleakness, a shadows choice

Neither sun nor breeze, nor bird in flight
To penetrate this, my saddened plight.
Yet from a corner deep within the soul
A voice whispered be free do not control

I listened, inhaled the pureness of breath
Stepping out from the darkened death
Soon life within me began to grow
As nature's surround began to glow.

With no reason that I could understand
I stood in a paradise that nature planned
My soul was empty, yet the world was grand
My heart devoid, a barren land
Yet all before me flourished fine
That which was barren was of my mind,

Beneath each rock

Beneath each rock I may search,
Along each coastal shore,
In meadows, valleys or mountain tops, neither here nor there shall I find.
It is not a mystery, nor is it hidden.
It is a truth, the only truth.
It is within and without all things; it has no name nor shape nor form,
Yet is the action of cause and effect.
It is the morning light, the moonlit sky; it is the food on which all life feeds.
How though is it hidden, if, it is so open?
How so, that I can neither see, nor hold it.
What is it that evades me? How am I to search for it, if it is not hidden?
That which is hidden yet is not, is that which remains when all else has been deducted
It is that which waits beyond the shadow of the veil.
Is it then, the nothing that I seek, the emptiness
the void, the before, before, before existed.
The first breath, the first sound, the first image.
Was it different then, was it other than, is now.
How did it formulate itself to be within itself? How did it become other than other?
To that which I seek once more, that which was once known yet now forgotten,
What is being without it, what worth this daily chore?

Consume me, me, and the earthly desires
that darken the path of life,
awaken this being from darkness that pure life may grow within.

Enough, enough of this folly, I seek to far and wide.
Though insanity may engulf me, I surrender unto the unknown.
For it is to be, for me to live, not for me to know.
To accept gratefully, my part within being.
To surrender to the way,
to release this overburdened mind of false instruction and desire.
Such riches as a simple raindrop are mine to reap with joy.
This then is my quest, the token of my being,
to live within all, as all lives within me as one, as one purpose shall flourish.
No evil, no right nor wrong,
neither judgement nor self-concern, for all is breathed by all.

Beyond all

Beyond all,
beyond that which has been,
where life flows only forward
The past washed away, leaving none but the erosion of time.
Tis here in the now, this very moment,
that choice of storm or calm is chosen.
To walk with the strength of sunlight within one's heart, or, that of bleakness.
To check, to be of; wisdom, of courage, of awareness,
of all that is within and around you.
To see, hear, feel.
to taste that of life, as it is lived.
To look upon others, as no more than travellers, seeking their own wisdom.
We as a one being, hold no control over the path of another,
and yet, rather than face the life we are given.
We seek to teach or to follow.
Yet the purity of truth, is to be ever grateful for.
Accepting what one has.
welcoming life, as an eternal gift.

Beyond the veil

Considering day with nature's own
Many succumb and are over grown
New life beckoning all the while
Each in its own facing strife and trial.
Whispers of wisdom a distant sound
Essence of being, so rarely found.
Purpose and value with shadows lie
Far beyond the veil of questions why?
Yet all is not lost, if one could find more
For the purest of self, shall always endure.

Blade of grass

In the pure divide, of all that is,
boundaries are set beyond
yet mind is fooled by a looking glass
what value this false perception.
How though to awaken soul?
But through eye and heart of truth.
where abides the essence of god-heart,
to lighten the darkest path.
What glory to touch one blade of grass,
to feel the pulsating of earths vein.
What wonder to behold the birth of spring
united with birth. Recycled.
Yet not of old, but refreshed and new,
birthed from the very first seed.
How many seeds though have since been sown,
in darkness on barren ground.
To know flight of bird or scurrying ant
To breathe life of the perfect world
To know thine self by root and passage.
clasping existence to thine breast.
yet why then exists, they of greed,
of folly toward heart and soul
darkening that of remaining course,
where sorrowful dreams await.
I am but a particle of this enormous space,
a wavering within essential time.
Yet what purpose can I serve,
if disconnected from the way
What then for each blade of grass....and I, and you, and them.

Broken fish.

Broken fish and scattered wine
A new turn of events, a change of time.
Lie of lies upon a hill
Black robed shadows in for the kill
Screaming down upon the crowds
broken bodies in bloody shrouds
As the son died and priests were born
The Badge of deception would soon be worn.

The stench of blood upon the cross
All humankind was at a loss
When a voice screamed down from the darkened sky
In sorrow and suffering you now shall die

Nether priest nor child shall understand
for they will be holding the devil's hand
2000 years of hypocrisy
2000 years of insincerity
2000 years of fear and lies
from bloodied priests the devils prize.
For 2000 years, a tale to tell
Leading, humanity on the path to hell.

But How

Strip down what is no longer useful. Awaken to your own beliefs
Prepare yourself for every eventuality
Listen and Watch with Understanding and Compassion
Be purposeful in your actions through mind-full meditations
Prepare organise and structure before the act
Be adaptable towards acts that appear suddenly
Increase your own awareness. Believe in your own strength
Allow your convictions the freedom to survive
Open yourself to the way. Change your life that, your truth is your way
and that, that which is false is diminished.
Organise, plan, be true, be steadfast. Be pure in spirit.
Harmonise with thy-self and bring strength to others.
Do not judge nor torment. Control your tongue and desires.
Prepare yourself each day. Be grateful with each evening.
Respect and honour what you believe.
Of nature, the gods, the path, the spirit, the seed.
Be pure in your thoughts and purposeful in your actions.
Do not operate from selfish needs or emotional torment
Awaken unto the word. Be true to the word
Follow the word of the natural spirit
Ever Increase your wisdom and knowledge
through the recognition of your true self.

By the hand

Let me take you by the hand and show you what's been planned.
Lead you through the streets of life, where there are they, creating the greatest strife.
Where people suffer in mental pain, though they, who seek no more than gain.
Let me take you on a magic tour, and show you beyond that darkened door
of mental madness and conspiracies, Indoctrinations and therapies.
Where you meet they, who for their own, execute powers and have overthrown
the way of compassion and sympathy, having no true knowledge of empathy.
For suffering is of little meaning to them, they that thrive through mental mayhem,
As they line their pockets with greed and pride
Through the many pills that they've supplied.

Just look around you, feel the pain, of the nameless ones condemned insane
of they who search, to freely breathe, upon god's earth, oh how, he must grieve.
Yet through this open and magic door we stand amongst the sick and poor
Within a society that confesses rights, yet still many homeless and lonely nights
How can there be such distorted truth, Upon this land beneath gods roof
For we are truth upon this earth and have been from our time of birth
and they who turned our minds astray shall surely come to rue the day
that they played God.

By the way of truth

By the way of life, by the way of truth
I walk without fear, for the freedom, Is, of natural existence.
Throughout time, the search becomes the point of direction.
Throughout time, the direction can become confused.
Throughout time, there is hope.
Throughout time, learning wisdom does not come easy.
Give unto oneself, time, for throughout time, there is truth.

Unto that which is not known
That, the essence of all
That which is the very seed all elements.
I raise my arms in gratitude for all that is placed within this realm.
In sorrow I bow my head,
for in ignorance do I use this life.
Wisdom and serenity, do I seek
yet in blindness have I travelled.
This misfortune is but mine alone
for I have not followed the golden path.

How many journeys are there to be
before I listen to life's true story.
Daily you place sustenance before me,
and offer nurture through natural cause.

What fool could walk away from, such grandeur
only one who hides from truth within shadows.

Unto that which is the very core of life
I lay my heart before you, that my pure originality be restored
to natures true, created form.
To be well with the way of, that which is. To ever be, in the moment.
To accept oneself as, a part of the world.
To see others as, a part of a whole.
To recognise that we are all, of the same seed.
Each with, the same needs, desires of happiness, of hopes, dreams
and a connection to that which, creates pure harmony and balance.
We each are seekers, and yet that very truth we seek
lies waiting within our very being, creatively longing, to be released.

Chasing Rainbows

Defeated, yet again, how sorrowful is this.
Fighting a battle that has no end.
There can be no pretence
The raging within, the turmoil, the shadow
Morning through day, through night
It isn't right
Any more
I have questioned, I have spoken.
I have spewed every word from my heart since first breath

But what care of my woes, my stories my tales, my life
For, is your life not as my life, when stripped to its barest form.
What of, the chasing of rainbows?
What of the utopian dream?
What purpose? what cause? what mean?
Raging torrents of obsessions, hurtle through this being,
ever searching, ever desiring, ever pushing forward into the unknown, from the unknown
for all that can be truly known, exists now, in this moment?
This moment exists, existed and has now passed.

Too late I missed it again
Time does not wait, nor, put life on hold but trudges on, through its own existence.
There is neither this, nor that, which shall hinder its existence, for it is, just is.
Having, neither that of form nor name.
Has no care, just is, now, the end of then, and, the beginning of that.
There is no gap, no in-between, just the continuum.
The unseen. The unknown.
That which surrounds the elements of nature's birth
Of air, of water, of earth and power of fire.
Of space, of energies, of that which is within and without.
Suddenly, I feel the insignificance of my form, of all it contains
amidst this creation of natural force.
Yet from where comes folly, false concepts, imaginations and prophecies?
On what is based, intelligence? What of command and instruction?

Unto all elements, of time, of energies and all that is,
I wonder, does the gull concern itself of the worm, or dare to question why?

Choice

With a new day, a new beginning,
Life anew appears
Each moment that passes, awaits each choice I may make
Without prejudice
My thoughts, my words, my actions; are the essence of my being...
Either I move forward with balance or imbalance,
The choice is always mine.
How I allow my mind to create, becomes the value of the outcome
Whether physical or emotional, the choice always remains mine
None other can be held responsible
As for the past, it has lived its term
and the future is unknown.
However, this moment of being exists
It is here in this moment that my choices and fate await.
That which is, will give unto me, that which I need
it is for me alone to accept with gratitude,
In the harming of none other.
So mote it be.

Could that it be different

And there I found life,
the very living of truth
that which I believed had deserted me so long ago,
Yet here it was deep in the heart of my very soul
The essence of me, the very creation that brought me to this point.
Oh, life how I love thee,
yet in return, give you no thanks for; the greatness you bestow around and within me,
I dishonour thee. I offer no true gratitude
for I am caught within mine own delusions.

Slave that I am, I bow before thee,
I could only wish to be in humility,
yet I know that pride and arrogance are ever there with me.

To ask forgiveness. is but the folly of; a fool,
who has no true understanding, nor, acceptance of the way.
Fool in ignorance I am,
For I know not the world, nor the value of,
Yet beyond my ignorance
is a great harmony that offers life beyond earthly knowledge.

Could that it be different,
your name be upon mine lips.
that the very vision of thee could be within mine sight.
Unto thee of day and night, creators of all elements,
may each simple breath I take be of thine grace.
I implore thee, recognise, see the trauma of mine days.
See how I have been so fooled by the words and actions of fools,
I become lost in mine way.
Yet I believe that you are in mine sight, my feelings my very being,
may it be that I lose thee not to the very evils of falseness and destruction.

Speak unto me,
lead me beyond this shadowed land of intolerance and foolhardiness
Awaken me I pray for as my life passes by, I see and regret
The imbalance, harmony and choice of true being
that through ignorance I have sadly missed.

Course of time

Throughout the course of time, life may renew its gift.
Once our human species have awoken to its own demise.
Never mind the false prophecies from they of power
For they are non-other than the germ of discontent.
No matter they who call upon gods,
For their ignorance shall one day unfold.
When the essence of truth shall again engulf
True purpose across the barren lands.
Tis then that nature, shall rise again
And the awakening of purest heart
Shall pierce the veil of ignorance,
no more to destroy the soul.

Crazy Mind

An excuse, reality or just a lie, accusations from finger pointing foe
Addiction stigma and labels, once spoken shall never go.
The making of empty promises, of martyrs in disguise.
of smooth tongues and fancy words, of deceit and open lies.
Ah but see them all so taken in, like flies, to a spider's trap,
all so simply gullible, across the global map.
How can they be trusted though? they who say they care,
for they have not a human clue, nor, experience to compare.
They have no way to be us, so how do they expect to know
the workings of a deranged mind and depressions that get so low.
I myself, search out answers. Twisted, tormented. perhaps insane,
wishing I could get another shot, at starting life again.
There is talk of health and well-being, of life change and great support
But within the heart of society, the weak become something to abort.

Of course, I know about responsibility. About awareness and self-change.
However, first there is this screwed up mind, I need to, re-arrange.
Yet what's the point, around and round, relapse, is not far way
and I will do the opposite of, everything I say.
Alone, no, I know I'm not, we are thousands by the score.
Each lost in, this hells paradise, that no animal could endure.
The mind, the mind, the crazy mind, for so many a living nightmare
Indoctrinated by those who so long ago, in their ignorance did not care,
until they found a purpose, a way to cure the sick
handing out the coloured pills, saying, 'this will do the trick'.
What a poor sad business, this industry of the mind
where money making capitalists, rob the vulnerable masses blind.
Ah, politics and religion, health and safety with screwed up rules,
the implantation of hypocrisy, that is spread within the schools.
So, what's the point, who gives a damn, about they, who are condemned
each suffering with no choice of life, in a world where, the powers pretend.
However, I have drifted from mine own story and crazy mind
or is it that, we are all screwed up, through the progress of our humankind.

Dark cold

Dark cold. Homeless, life dreary
alone, forgotten...just tired and so weary
empty pockets ... emotions forlorn,
there must be more, for which I was born.
Day time brings pain, more hunger and thirst,
what life is this, with which I am cursed
Awakened with nature, no tears can be shed,
For this is my journey, who knows, what waits ahead
Roads passing roads, village and town,
scavenging for food, find a place to lie down.
Alcohol becomes medicine, both for body and brain
other substances and gambling, out to destroy me again.
Life on the road, just nowhere to turn…
…that I live a day longer, is the greatest concern.
How soon come the day,
I wished not to die?
having to fight for my life, ever questioning, why?
I follow the path, I stumble I fall,
Ever waiting to hear, that sweetened call,
'come home, be at peace, for we shall console
Tis here you shall find nurture and love for your soul.
Till then, continues the journey, in hope that my strength grows,
and where it may lead to, my god only knows.
However, tis my place, to strive, thrive and survive
For life is life is life, is worth it, to fight, and stay alive.

Deception

Oh deception, what art though, from where do you originate.
How is it that you can reach unto every being?
How is that that you so easily capture, the natural being and blind it from actuality?
It is a sadness that for what we are created, we are not
That this great deception eats into us from the beginning of time.

What wonder, would I see, feel, hear and be
if deception had no place within my life force.
From where comes the ability to destroy the essence of mine own being.
For it had no existence, before that moment of conception
before the darkness of deception was laid upon me

If I could but travel back in time, to that precious second before birth
to capture the fleeting moment of; my true essence
to know of its knowledge, of its true purpose.
of its greater wisdom to deny, they, the bringers of deception.

If I could but know of these things. I search, yet know not
Only that within the very depths of my soul, is a cry of truth.
I have seen my deception and its darkness.
That ever-flowing veil, that keeps hidden the purity of things.

Do not deny me the part, you play in this deception.
Hear your own voice. See the gains that you and I strive for.
Is this truly what we are, what we have become
Are we truly a species of deception, labeled under many false names.

Even the truths that we may believe, that we place upon another
becomes yet another, deceptive breath.

Could we but change the course of time, free from desirc and greed
If we could carry but one truth from beyond birth
Would we still live such lies, or, shine from?
The greater essence of our true being.

Deepest soul

There are many avenues toward well-being
Many causes to change one's life
Yet what suits one may not suit another
For each are prone to, their own vice or strife.

Being human though is no easy task
Mixed emotions the enemy within
With ever the need and desire for more
Becomes a battle we rarely win.

Yet should you stop a while, prepare thine self
Allowing self-worth of life be true
You may discover that of deepest soul.
ever watching over you.

Do not doubt, nor ponder long
For life soon passes by
Tis better that you live your life
Than ever questioning why.

Destination

Inspirational destination
Next stop
Judgement day…
…. Come what may

Today, so they say,
is of great importance.
So was yesterday…
…however, that has passed.
Tomorrow is but a plan
Of unknown outcome,
Hope for just some.
No…. for all.
Yet destiny, fate and the other world
may not always be, in agreement.

Destination happiness.
Sorry, no such stop.
Just a fleeting moment,
Soon to pass.
Destination sadness
Each stop along the way
Platforms for Greed, envy, anger and desire,
For some the search for joy.

Destination contentment
Being one with the value of being
Accepting all as one with all
Next stop harmony and balance surround.

Disorder of the will.

Disorder through external influences

Disorder, the lack of clarity, of ability to move forward,
to make a choice based on the actuality of one's own experience

The powerful influencing of society, that brings about the demeaning of true character.

Where is, balance, where is harmony, can it be seen, or felt.
Do we give permission for the will to be unshaded?
Or is there a preference toward deviation from normality.

What is normal, the way of things.
The pure essence of originality, the natural essence of life that flows.

No matter our desires or dreams,
we as a species can never own life,
nor interfere with the harmony of nature.
Nor can we tame it.

Yet we ourselves, and only through our selves,
can determine and accept that, we are of nature,
of existence and of simple being.

We are not Gods and have neither the knowledge, nor wisdom of.
We can but live, our personal beginning and ending of times.

We have no right to make claims
or to influence, or, to cause any form of destruction in any way.

And yet we do so each waking moment.

I can but hope that today, I live with clarity.
Aware of the many false witness that I may inherently bare.
May, what be beyond, allow me the grace
and recognition of, mine own ignorance.
That I may create order from that of my truest nature
And not that of disorder created through mine own will.

Dispute

It has all been said before.
By someone else.
Way back in time.
Repetition. Repetition. Repetition.
Truth, discovered, over, and over again.
And, shall continue to be so throughout our times

Today, a new truth, which though may be old, and maybe, not true.
Tomorrow yet another discovery. making yesterday's truth, no more than, a fable

Mentality reality
Yours, or, the dreams of another.
Falsifying testament, for the sake of, one moment of ego,
The overpowering need for, self-acclaim.

Distorted words blown out of proportion, statements of power.
Of greed, desire and claiming of affinity
Yet what is known, is not. As neither was it before.

That there is truth, is a truism undoubtedly so.
Yet not in the face of realism.

How strong the desire, to say, we know?
Transportable wisdom shared,
Yet with the power to shatter the dreams of another.
For one person's gospel, could well be the downfall of another.

Therefore, there is much to question of our world and its past
of Adam, Joseph Johns and Mary's
Mohammed, Krishna and Buddhas to name but a few,
It has all been said before but can never be a given, without dispute.
For that is the hidden knowledge of the absolute.

Dreams and desires

Ever seeking, desires. Addictions even, or that we believe to be pleasure.
yet pleasure or disaster, is this not suffering perhaps, pain, the inner suffering we seem to enjoy
What foolishness we promote to feel alive, what delusions we so easily create.
In the name of satisfaction, we endlessly become jokers of life is self.
Oh, Foolish ones, be true, face yourself for the mockery you lay at your own feet.
Judge yourself, be honest in your words.
For you know the wrongs you commit against yourself.
yet onward you fight, as though an envious enemy.
Unknowing of your own mind one minute to the next.
Torment and loneliness you rain upon your own head.
Then in ignorance and false pride you stand.
Your ego ripping at your very soul.
Your own shadow laughing in your face. When will you awaken?
See the folly of your ways.
When will you on bended knees, see yourself for, the lost spirit you have become.
Lies like flies multiplying, creating black clouds within your dreams
Not one day of honor do you live unto yourself.
Blind conceited and foolish, the dance of devils, your daily right.
How long this song of lament?
Awaken to the trickery, the mirages you create with childish gloom
Awaken Fool awaken, open your eyes, your heart, your spirit, your soul.
Awaken the truth and wisdom that lays forever dormant,
having you believing that, truth is but a forbidden light.
How you suffer and blame? How you cheat and cry?
How you look at the emptiness that surrounds you?

See how you hide, In your own pretense world of non-satisfaction.

Or maybe you have a greater wish
That you may awaken anew, afresh with what you know.
For you are more, than just a shadow. You are far more than just a fool…

.. You are wise
The years have taught you of, the heart of life
Listen to the wisdom that begs you to step out of this darkness in which you shroud yourself.
Throw down the cross, release yourself from the thorns
And live, yes live as a true being. Live as nature would live…..

….. Live as truth would live.
Allow life to bring; harmony, balance and contentment to your being
Awaken, for the earth is never far from you, ever waiting for your space to fill.
Remorse after death would be a sad thing. Such unrest for eternity
So, awaken now even if you must die the morrow Least be, but for one day, one hour, one moment, true to thine own being.
Distance yourself from the darkness of self-pity and sorrow
Feel the warmth and pureness of your life's blood
as it pulsates gently through your living body.

Defining the self

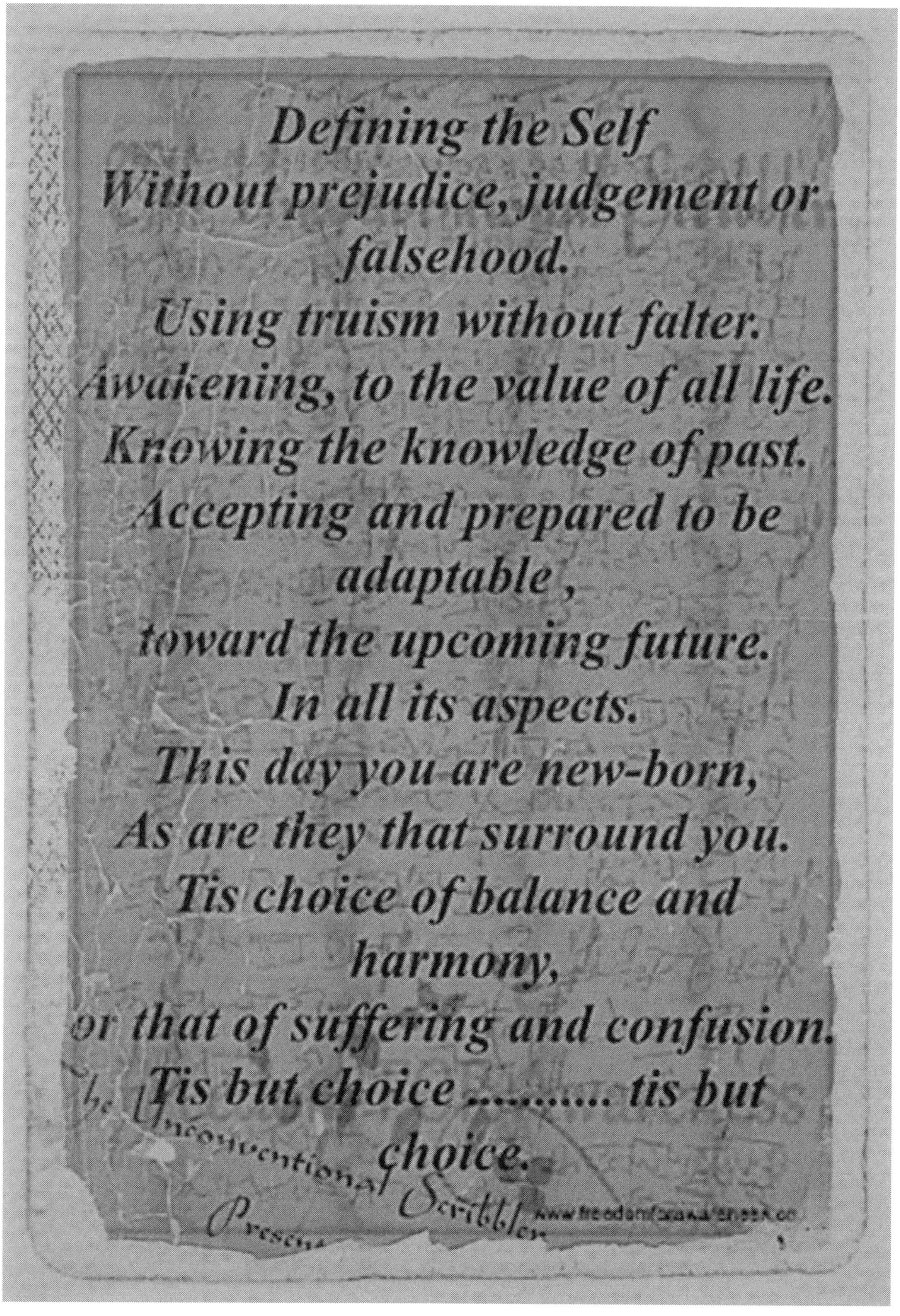

Defining the Self
Without prejudice, judgement or falsehood.
Using truism without falter.
Awakening, to the value of all life.
Knowing the knowledge of past.
Accepting and prepared to be adaptable ,
toward the upcoming future.
In all its aspects.
This day you are new-born,
As are they that surround you.
Tis choice of balance and harmony,
or that of suffering and confusion.
Tis but choice .... tis but choice.

Elements

Through love of life and being. Through truth of soul and warmth
The journey for discovery, comes upon us each new day.

For life, this life, this only life
This single life we know.
Ever offers gifts from natures hand
Whispering wisdom within the winds

Why take the path of suffering?
That true essence be left behind
Why allow that of ignorance
Seep through the boundaries of time.

Truth of being ever waits for us
To step forth from within the dream
That we may perceive the purpose of
Our nature within nature's own

Yet heartless we become unto the self
therefore, heartless unto our kin
Dispassionate fools with blinded eyes
hidden behind darkened clouds

For mine own I cry, 'awaken fool',
Hear your own being within your soul
hide not in waste of precious time
for death bells are soon to toll.

Imagine, dream, reach out your heart
Open self to the living spirit
For the elements of the great design
Offer knowledge from far beyond

Be not deaf to the voice of truth
That soar throughout the lands
For if not as one with nature's breath,
but dust in the wind, would we remain.

Equality of each

Who am I to judge
what right do I have to investigate your mind.
I have no right, nor do I know your mind,
How could I.

Tis true that many experiences are of like.
Good, bad, indifferent, traumatic, deceptive and more
Health, wealth, poorness, sadness, a cacophony of emotions
Maybe we have met,
maybe we have fought each other in a battle of wits, or just plain survival
We may have been lovers, or warriors, destroyers or builders.
Whatever, we could no more than, our own individual being.

Our own thoughts demanding satisfaction and outcomes to suit our needs.
rightly or wrongly we may have instructed the other, made demands, been insistent,
critical or dogmatic.
Whoever, whatever, wherever, the option remains, to have hope of heart
and demand for that of; survival.

The desperate need to; belong, behold, to contain. the human right of harmony
Yet with human right, there is that of betrayal, as the human wrong of ignorance,
living by guess work, false teachings, surrounded by them
wanting only dominance over another.
Can it be, that we are so foolish not to have faith in our own gifted life.
To not recognize the equality of each and their own.

Eradicating Ignorance

What is expected, where is mind,
why are there thoughts floating around that have neither rhyme nor reason.
What is reality, what is purpose. Why such fallacy. Does morality exist?
Is there a god? Is there independent life, is love a false emotion?
A confusion of words. lost in the meaningless dictionary of all languages.
Why is one person of more worth than another?
Who knows if, they who profess their connection to god, are not sufferers of mental illness spreading no more than their own deceptions around them
What of religions, policies and laws that suit one and not the other. Who is to say that the law is correct when it is changeable and so often corrupt? Who is to say that the church is not the work of evil?
This life is so confusing, full of deceit and illusions. How can one truth be a truth and another truth be a lie. Who has the right to demand, who has the right to rebel?
Show me the rule book, not fables written by human hand. Show me the book of rules that comes with birth, not the indoctrinations of elders who never found the reality of pure harmony.
How sad the cloud of ignorance that leads to, that of; misconceptions, delusions and fabricated stories. All for no more than, the gain of power, of rule, of governance and greed.
So here I share my delusions for do I not have the right to speak as any other upon this earth.
As do they of all nations, believing they are of special power upon this earth,
Though not all are messengers of purpose nor tranquillity.
We can but hope, that just as that of the common cold, or a form of parasite that causes discomfort, a cure shall be found, *eradicating, ignorance, greed and lies from the foolishness of, the human mind.*

Escaping negativity

How easily issues draw us into negativity.
Soon forgotten, moments of contentment and serenity.
How easily dark demons of the past can arise?
turning the slightest trigger into chaos.
Yet nothing has altered your true self.
Your inner being is still there,
even if it has not come to full fruit,
Why allow trivia and negativity displace you.
For If you can remain aware that there is far more to your life
that the issues presenting themselves are by far inferior to,
the true value of your life.
To believe in, the pure essence of your inner self
Can bring about far greater endurance….
.. Keeping negativity of past, present and future at bay.

Eternal

You called me from that restless sleep
You took me down to rivers deep
Where the setting sun gave way to the moon
With the ebbing tide whispering the secrets of time
Like a ragged man before you
I weep
my soul ever sinking beneath the sands of broken souls
The nightmares arrive, I call your name
Echoing far away in shadowed caverns
A time long past, a devil's curse heavy upon my soul.
the grass was once greener, the shadows lighter
more than just an empty shell of darkness.
Awaken me, stir me from this vision
for I turn restlessly towards the awaiting grave of night

Allow me escape, from this mirage.
For too long have I been here.
I am tired, let sanity be my friend one more time
Allow me that I may Move on now
To Leave. To Turn. To love. To Move. To Live
To have life, My life.
I am calling Time. I am heading home
I feel the world opening her eyes
I Feel my soul stretching out
I awaken. I Touch down. I am home
Your shadow grows dimmer, fainter
Your name echoing far away, time is nigh
let this be the last, the letting go. The last sigh.
The warmth of the eternal essence.

Extraordinaire

Life extraordinaire
Folly, folly, folly.
Of ignorance, remain aware.

Of whom, or, what, even why
purpose need be found
Tis surely true, tis but a while
before placed beneath the ground,
where not even a withered hand
shall find a pure heart to hold
Yet worry not, for loss nor gain
nor fret o'er heat or cold.

folly, folly, folly
of ignorance, remain aware
embrace your essence of being
let go the extraordinaire.

Of whom, or what, or even why
tis of contentment that need be sought
worry not of the when or how
Care not for desirous thought.
feel, hear, see, touch
feel your truth within
care, share, be aware
Allowing wise mind to begin

Ah the essence of being.
The wonder of life aware
No folly greed or sadness.
For I seek not the extraordinaire.

Family

I am, mine own mother, mine own father and mine own friend.
Yet of three. there can be no trust

For failings of inaptitude leaves me floundering throughout,
The lack of nurture that I attend upon myself
The lack of care, no need of attention.

What family is this I belong, allowing me to stray
Beyond barriers of wellbeing
What false instruction is laid upon me?
That Confuse me within myself.

Alas, how can I ever be freed for my own instructions
When I continue to bring about mine own destructions

Does it need be this way?
Could it not be, that we live in harmony?
Entreated with love care compassion and wisdom.

By myself do I battle. each waking day and yet
I so long for the warmth and worth of my own being.

This family to which I belong are all that I have
Only trust will bond us into one
Therefore, I need be a strong father
A loving mother, a devoted child and trusted friend
If It is my desire to truly understand
the harmony of mine self, and, this world.

Fish out of water

How then, am I to survive, for there is no control
Everything slips away into darkness,
People see me, they hear me but know not of me
I flounder like a fish out of water
I cry into the night stars, I drift with the tumbling winds
I feel them laughing at my stories
Yet they don't hear the true story I am telling
what is this punishment. Am I a fallen angel?
Is there no moment of reform? need I die every day?
Is anyone listening? Do they even care?
That waking of the morning or sleep of the night, I remain
Like a floundering fish out of water.
With no helping hand, I shall die upon dry ground
What love, what care, what open value of living a life
Whom knows my pain who feels my loss?
Am I just a mirage? An echo in the wind A ghost of non-existence.
I remember once, as a child, seeing the world as a place of wonder
Know I wonder where that world went
I speak to angels who hide in shadows, I cry to goddesses beyond the clouds
I break down the barriers only to find eemptiness beyond
On bended knees I whisper to the wonders of all nature
Why can I not live as you. To take each breath as a flower. To stand tall as a tree.
To shine as within the rays of the sun.
To be a beam of wisdom within the moons angelic beam.
Oh, precious life why am I forsaken, why torn from life's nurture,
living within, extinction of time.
Yet though I reach into the heart of all being, thirst and hunger remain my way.
Though still I believe for this is not how it is meant to be.
One day my last breath shall be taken
The long sleep shall become mine world
Having not known the purpose of the journey before.
Is there no beginning, before I find the end?
As a floundering fish out of water, shall I pass on
And even should, that helping hand be there, mine time shall have passed
And all that I have seen, within natures grace, shall be lost to me.
For I could not hear its call, nor see the purity, all was but a shadow of desire.
Maybe, as I float throughout heavens skies, the truth shall be opened unto to me
And love shall pierce my soul, the loneliness shall be forgotten
And should it ever be, that I return
My heart of love shall spread, to all who flounder, like fish out of water.

Folly

See the folly of your ways
When will you on bended knees
See yourself for the traitor that you may be

Lies like flies multiplying, creating black clouds within your dreams
Not one day of honour do you live unto yourself?
Blind conceited and foolish the dance of devils your daily right
How long now you fool
How long this song of lament
Awaken fool to the trickery
The mirages you create with childish gloom
Awaken Fool awaken
Open your eyes, your heart your spirit, your soul,
Awaken this being that lays forever dormant
Believing truth, to be a forbidden light.

How you suffer and blame
How you cheat and cry
How you look at the emptiness that surrounds you

See how you hide
In this pretence little world of non-satisfaction

Or maybe you have a greater wish
That you may awaken anew, afresh with what you know
For you are more, than just a shadow
You are more than just a fool
You are wise
The years have taught you, the heart of life
Listen now to the wisdom within
that begs you to step out of this darkness in which you shroud yourself
Throw down the cross
Release yourself from the thorns
And live, yes, live as a true being
Live as nature would live
Live as truth would live
Allow life to bring; harmony, balance and contentment to your being
Awaken fool for the earth is not far from you
ever waiting for your space to fill.
Remorse after death would be a sad thing………..

Folly

……….. such unrest for eternity
So, awaken now. even if you must die the morrow.
Least be, but for one day, one hour, one moment
true to thine own being.
Distance yourself from the darkness of self-pity and sorrow
feel the warmth and pureness of your life's blood as it pulsates through your living body
In heart
In mind
In soul
In spirit
In being
Allow the essence of your true existence
Welcome you with open arms.

Fool

When feeling down, when feeling blue
I conjure up an image of you.
When the days not right and there is no light
I give into love and your face so bright.

When in darkest dreams I can find no peace
I whisper your name that the loneliness cease
and though you appear as true as the day
I know when I awake you will have gone away.

If Dreams are for fools, then a fool I shall be
carrying your name in the heart of me
if dreams are for fools then I would rather remain
a fool that's in love, yeah, I know it's insane.

I conjure you up wherever I go
it's crazy I know, but I just can't let you go
I carry you with me through night and through day
I'm not such a fool to send you away

If Dreams are for fools, then a fool I shall be
carrying your name in the heart of me
if dreams are for fools then I would rather remain
a fool that's in love, yeah, I know it's insane.

For cause of want

For cause of want
For cause of need
Ever consumed
with material greed.

For cause of love...
For cause of hope
Ever with emotions
Of life to cope

For cause of freedom
For cause of self
Ever fearing death
and states of health.

For cause of life
For cause of soul
searching the unknown
for want of control

For cause of the will
For cause of the heart
Accepting what is
is the best place to start.

For Today

For today I shall
Provide myself with my needs
before my desires
I shall endeavor to be adaptable and flexible always
Yet remaining steadfast in my wellbeing.
Daily I shall recognize the importance of
my existence and existence of others.
As I reap my rewards, so shall I be generous,
When that of my own house is in order.
I shall appreciate the skills that I possess,
always willing to learn more.
I shall accept the laws of the land. so long as,
they harm not me. nor another.
I shall remain at peace with my god
And allow others to be at peace with theirs.
I shall always recognize, respect, and remain aware
that nature is not only a greater force than I
but also sustains my life.

For you are the Rainbow

Tell me who can I love, tell me what I can do.
where can I go, when life turns darkened blue?
who can I call, tell me what I should say
when colour becomes absent, from my waking day.

I have but to close my eyes and clearly think of you
And slowly you shall appear to me, through mists of orange hue
I picture you, for you are, the rainbow of my life
You break away the shadows, you take away the strife.
You become the cherished bloom of spring and the daffodil
my rainbow of many colours above a sun lit hill.
you make me want to laugh, to hear natures chorus sing.
For you are the many colures that only a rainbow could bring.

Tell me who can I love, tell me what I can do.
where can I go, when life turns darkened blue?
I have but to close my eyes and clearly think of you
And slowly you shall appear to me, through mists of orange hue

Just knowing that there is rainbow ever watching over me
brings radiance of life and perfect harmony
a rainbow of all seasons, a wonderous image in the sky
that makes me want to laugh and sing and never question why?
For you are the Rainbow

I have but to close my eyes and clearly think of you
And slowly you shall appear to me, through mists of orange hue
I picture you, for you are, the rainbow of my life
You break away the shadows, you take away the strife.
You become the cherished bloom of spring and the daffodil
my rainbow of many colours above a sun lit hill.
you make me want to laugh, to hear natures chorus sing.
For you are the many colures that only a rainbow could bring.

Forgive me, if I deny you

Forgive me, if I deny you
If I have no wish to believe your point of view
for I hear not one word that resonates with original essence
only stories of something past.
Might I ask who taught you your perception?
What facts did you unearth within?
Though perhaps it is safer to go with inspiring flow
What though of the actual, of natural
what of life's creation without false selection
Forgive me my questions of disbelief
Truly I want to understand your view
but I have heard this view on other tongues, both for, against, and amiss.
Be not offended that I do not bow down to your way of reckoning,
This is not of morals, nor of right nor wrong
nor prejudice nor love, nor hate, nor peace.
Who pray tell me am I, to say of, or, to question your very word
when there are others who follow the same path as yourself.
I remain aside of all, accepting the pureness of nature's own.
Could it be that the cleverer we become? the more to lose our spirit.
Of what spirit, I know not,
for to know the unknown, I need seek a clearer mind.

Fortune can be mine wisdom

So, am I to be beaten again,
by addiction or some other product of defeat.
From without, or, within.
Throughout history the many have sought to discover purpose,
only to leave fabrication in place of; the perfection of just being,
of accepting, of living in the appropriate moment.
accepting that, needs will be met.
Do we need live the life of a hermit? denounce one's own rights and welfare,
or, just be alive in harmony with, the truth of that which is.
Alas, this is not allowed to be
for the cloud that over power the brain is far too great
to demand, the actual right, as a living being, to find harmony and peace in natural existence.
I do not, cannot accept that, the mystical wonder of life is nonexistent.
I demand my freedom of knowledge and wisdom,
my universal right to be connected to that which is.
No, I am not able to name this wonder because of some law beyond my bounds.

Darkness be gone,
take away these false negative emotions that you distort my mind with.
I denounce your falsehoods, Yet I shall embrace your truth,
I shall no longer sit back and allow the wonder of life to be destroyed through shadowed ignorance.
I awaken the light within me.
I stand for my true being and purpose.
Be gone your blackness, take your lies and confusions elsewhere.
I demand my life,
I demand instruction for my life.
I am here, I was given birth, and now I want the freedom to live out and be.
Allow me this, speak to me of; my purpose and how I lighten this veil of blindness,
I refuse to accept that this world is dark and purposeless.
I listen out for thine instruction, I seek thy calling
yet I seek not your name nor holiness,
only truth of the path laid out in all that is natural
that which is pure within its own essence.

Deny me no longer, I have paid for my ignorance ten-fold,
I have repented my foolishness and incapability's, recognizing only that
the path can be made clear,
Fortune can be but mine, that Wisdom ever lighten my path.

Getting it right

A simple question, of what is true
For all we seek, and all we do.
Of living well without remorse
Of how to follow the most natural course
The simplest answer has neither name nor form
Of purest purpose for which we're born
Yet on we strive in hope of gain
Desires and greed bringing naught but pain.
In sorrow setting ourselves apart
From that which is the truth of heart.
In judgement we Condemn, so full of pride
Tis here we create the great divide
For humanity chose to ignore
The greater purpose our world is for.

God doesn't live here

God doesn't live here anymore,
as nor do any other of whom we believe to be all powerful.
for I doubt that they abide the desecration and destruction of natural creation.

Make believe and egoistic fallacies became an embarrassment, so,
they just up and withdrew, saddened by the ignorance of the human race.

It is understandable though, when you look deep into the simple guidelines given
and the lack of ability to comply.

As for the divides, the wars, indoctrinations and false actions
carried out in their names, there could only be disgust.
For that which provided the spiritual essence, were ever betrayed
by them, with whom they shared wisdom.

It is not that they no longer care, but can no longer be within the heart of mankind, for
to many rules have been broken, to many lies created.

Yet still we call out in hope,
still we blame the gods for all wrongs,
yet the blame is of own construction
for is we who have falsified the way of instruction
to suit our own needs, 'tis we who in our greed and foolishness have created our
gullibility.

That which is, the spirit and soul of life, had no choice but to take a step back,
Whilst we the bearers of humanity ever continue to destroy that which is given
That which is can but wait in hope, that there will be they
who once again can connect and listen, without vanity and egoistic cause.

The desecration shall one day end, but, until that day, it is sad to say
God in all its form, doesn't live here anymore.

God Who

Of god, tell me of this god.
Tell me of it now, not a thousand nor two thousand nor that of more.
Tell me of his name three thousand years ago or even ten.
Tell me the meaning of the name 'god' tell me of its form, of gender and such.
Tell me of the wars, the pestilence, the diseases and tortures against one's own.
Tell me of celebrations, of rituals for desire and greed.
What though of; grace and harmony within
Fools, lost in past eras, creating the same sufferings into the present...
What are we but mere germs of life.
Parasite even, feeding of the life of others
Speak to me of god, such hypocrisy, actor's, jesters of time.
For what little is known of the purpose being, nor the how, nor why.
What value, living in reflection of a past, no longer understood
Life bought to none, but sad `destruction.
The many great causes, no more than a fallacy of pretence, all for greater glory.
How can I address you, when you know not, that your cause is no longer understood and now been long forgotten?
Oh, truth of time, if only you could reach into the foolishness of they who live now, they, who have become indoctrinated with cross purpose.
How pretentious the art of worship, even that of education is a mockery,
unto they who know.
The gods we know not,
Nor how we came upon the earth.
What pity do or can the 'gods have, when the true essence of the wisdoms are no longer lived.
It is but for the individual to awaken, to become more than fools, petty creatures lost to the presence of ignorance.
Once our cause was true, nature provided nurture and the universe fed us with simple wisdoms that our species may survive.
We made many mistakes
the greatest………. turning our backs on the way of things.
Yet still we remain led by teachers not such of wisdom but greater fools than yourselves.
what words can I say
Were it my place I would invoke you remember, they who have passed in sufferance of gods of men.
Allow the gods freedom to be the essence of all things, not portrayed in form, name or gender.
accept god as is…of which we know not.

Gods will

Beyond darkness, beyond curves of light
Beyond rising peaks, beyond human sight
Beyond perils way, to the far beyond
I wonder shall I discover
a world that corresponds,
to paradise.

Beyond the splinter lies the dust
Beyond the needle only rust
Beyond my bones a carrions meal
When all has gone
Will god reveal?

How Eden turned sour upon the devil's tongue
Not long after life begun
However, if true why continue the seed
That is said to have made us an evil breed
Twice not thrice have I questioned myself
For thrice may overpower the truth of health
Perhaps the answer is a knowledge unknown
Or perhaps a mind so overblown
The perfect question but a mythical tale
Leaving gods own will to prevail.

Gone the Angel of purity

Tis in sufferance that mankind lives
ignorant of their true being.
Lost in a mindset of fallacy and fantasy
unknown the pure wonders of life.
Where man turned against woman
woman against man
woman against woman
man, against man.
Each new soul born of innocence led into torment and that of, false existence.
Gone the angel of purity, lost the connection of divine essence
forgotten the true purpose of given life.
Leaving only a path of selfishness to walk exploited by; pride, greed and envy.

How then, can peace be found?
How can, love abide, whilst the blood boils with anger
and each soul remains enveloped with dis-array and rage.
I bow my head in shame for am I not guilty of blindness to the way of things
am I not also of the mindless and dis-satisfied a prisoner of fabrications.
Yet it is for me to recognize the corruption of mine own mind
To live with mine own truths not making judgement upon the ways of another.
Yet truth seems long time lost cast into darkness and un-rest.
Where freedom of spirit remains surrounded by shadows,
and inner soul laden with disbelief.

How the light and divine essence must scorn our defiled ways.
As daily we are guilty of abusing, the purposeful life of, natural originality.
Perhaps the day shall come when in unity we shall awaken as one
with the very spirit of our living souls enjoined within the truth of, natures course.

Goodbye

Here I sit, one of the many, perhaps one of the few
Who am I to know? What am I to do?
I want to share, yet share what
For I only have what the others have *Self-perception in a jar*
I would like to give. However, nothing is mine
Only that which sits upon an empty stage.
I would like to hold happiness in my hand. Perhaps blow it far and wide
Yet if I do, who shall share the dreams, other than I.
Being alive is enough for me, and yet
I feel dissatisfaction, for the peace I seek
Is beyond this mortal mind.
Ah freedom I scream, awaken to me
Give me sails and mighty winds
That unto paradise I may sail….
…. Yet my heart denies all dreams.
What words are there to utter? For they are words from forlorn lips
A drifter within a typhoon storm of A fool, with no star to guide.
Ah heaven, are you paradise?
Oh hell, are you of, Eden's path?
What part of this is neutral ground?
What love that's never found.
Harmony never dies, nor peace, nor, love, nor need, nor kind
May I speak of thee in but a word? *Goodbye, goodbye, goodbye.*

Grasping at a life.

Grasping at a life seeking the originality of pure thought
not trusting my own perceptions, therefore, why should I trust the perceptions of others
Words of wisdom have been laid before us, however, it is only through that of ego
that truth becomes shadowed to suit our personal value and desires.
To speak of God; to even utter this word is a conception beyond our consciousness.
For, that which is sought, has no name, nor form, nor image and yet persistently we create that which is of no creation.
Alas I know not the answer, for the question is far beyond my knowledge.

Attachment, the holding on to that which does not belong,
all things have a place elsewhere and shall always be governed by the freedom of motion.
Nothing can be mine as it could belong to another. It is within itself and has no rightful place of permanence, nor that of component parts for they too are ever within, their own motion and time.
Therefore, never can one part belong to the other.
Motion and time never cease, just as the primal essence shall never cease, or belong in one mode of time, for it continuously flows through, around and within all things.

What then can I call mine, what can I claim as mine.
Even my thoughts cannot be of me, as, I cannot contain them, they change and move, there is no grasping, for if I seek to grasp, to own, they will filter away leaving a void that contains no conception of that which shall become….

…Perhaps it is the void, the unknown to which I belong.
Is it that I should remain in stillness knowing of neither right nor wrong, allowing motion and time to deliver only that which I need know.
yet what of my need, to own, to personalize with labels, for how can others know what is of mine, or what is theirs.
How can we share that which passes through us, in ever continuous motion?

And therefore, lays my sadness, my plethora of emotions, yet if I cannot own them, am I not just grasping at a life that is beyond mine own being.

Gratitude

Everything I receive is a gift, to appreciate and treasure,

for if a gift is not treasured, then for what purpose would it exist.

Each moment is a gift and if that moment cannot be treasured, then what purpose of that moment.

Each thought is a gift, if it is not treasured, then what purpose the thought.

All things in life are a gift of life, the body, mind (soul),

if they are not, then what purpose can they serve

All outcomes are a gift, positive to gain, negative to learn

What purpose any gift if not accepted with grace and wisdom.

How sad that the many gifts are taken for granted and discarded without thought.

It is sorrowful that all gifts bestowed become neglected, without recognition or care.

Is it but a fool who could act in this manner, then tis I who is a fool,

a child with no knowledge of life, how could I alone be so ungrateful for the many wonders

am I therefore still a child without light or understanding.

No, I am neither fool nor child

For I clearly see that to be devoid of gratitude, selfish in ignorance. asleep and blind to truth of being.

Then shall even my grave serve no purpose, nor bring peace.

Heaven knows why

Heaven knows why
However, I do not
Heaven knows why
Perhaps I forgot
Forgot what
What's to forget?
Heaven knows why
And I find this a threat
A threat to my sanity
In all that I try
For something is missing
Heaven knows why
Love gained, love lost
A foolish man's pride
Devoured by his ego
Unbalanced inside
Bearing the brunt
Of his mindless mishaps
Heaven knows why
He gets caught in such traps
If heaven knows why
Then I deserve to know also
For why there should be secrets
And stories untrue
Some mental deficiency
That affects me and you
I have not the answer
I was born and shall die
Yet the purpose of my existence
Maybe heaven knows why.

How hungry the world over?

How hungry the world over?
For the want of love
the need of companionship.
To give and receive
To be somewhere else
To be someone else
To be able to do something different.

How hungry the world over
That desire for more
To seek and judge
To condemn and forget
To maim and kill
To imprison and enslave.

How hungry the world over
To have one moment of self-worth
Of understanding
Of awareness
Of an inner self connection
Of knowing that we are one
the world over.

How sad my world

How sad my world, that I can judge and condemn the lives of others
Who am I to believe that I contain the wisdom of life?
Who am I to be deaf to the needs of others?
Who am I really?
I am not you, I can never be so
However, I can know better, for I am my own god
Or I can conform to the many beliefs of others
And feel correct in my assumptions for I shall be one of many
Tis a sorrow that I am so blind to the truth
Ever seeking yet never knowing.
Yet here I rest looking out at the folly of so many lives,
If only they could be me
Then they would know all that I know
They too could be gods unto themselves
They too could have the right to judge and condemn
How grateful I am for my greatness
For my selfishness and arrogance
For where I would be
Without my pride and purity
Who other than I, can show the true path
I am wisdom itself
I am the path and instructor of all that is.
How you should bow before me
Recognize the importance of my being
Forget your own pathetic ways
You and they are all but fools wandering aimlessly
Forever lost
Hearken unto me and life shall be greater than you could ever desire
Hearken unto me and you shall discover your own true self
As though you were writing this from your own heart
Think of these words as a mirror, allow them to reflect Honesty
Perhaps truthful humility is the answer.

How to be as one

Feel that spectacular moment when, you are one with you.
Acceptance of self-worth in all that you do.
In harmony with all that surrounds
a wonderful balance in all that abounds
That fleeting moment, when all elements fill your soul
That nurture of Earth, of air, fire and water, so beyond your control.
That perfect harmony between flower and bee
the golden mean in all that you see.
That essential moment when nature your senses
Breaking through the dullness, of darkened defences.
When your heart and soul shines as rays of the sun
Transferring you to a time when all essence was one
When you breathe in the moon and feel the peace of night
Her thousand eyes shining bright
When you feel each beat of our worlds loving heart
Then of harmony and balance you never shall part.
Yet only from within and your desire to connect
Can you discover a world so harmoniously perfect?

I am mine own being

Spirit of earth,
the beginning, the way forward and all which is beyond
we are given spirit of life, yet how easy it is to become blocked from the reality of our own existence, through lack of natural reasoning.
How sad that value and purpose becomes closed from the truth in life's early stage, the true spirit taken over by, ignorance of other beings, who themselves have lost the way,
However, ridding the many indoctrinations and false wisdoms is never a journey of simplicity. yet is not beyond repair,

Living with false emotion can become the greatest barrier
hiding that of true essence.
Tis possible one may find a true guide
Yet to reach the realm of true presence. There is the need of; strength, courage and fortitude
For to discover just a small spark within one's own being, unbiased self-awareness.is called upon
Wondrous spirit of purest time awakens this being that the truth unfolds.

That no longer there be contempt of life.
Bring Thee now forward that the ghost of self-destruction, be gone,
and none but the purest of words be heard.
Pass thine self through the hoop of truth that false knowledge be stripped bare,
That the true self that may live ever more in peace.

No longer the child, nurtured as an empty bowl but fed with truth, far from mortal's mind.
Be gone thee of memory, be gone of evil ways, for you are not of truth nor peace, nor harmony, nor, sweet serenity's peaceful ways
Be gone now yea lovers curse, be gone you son of greed
Be gone you of hypocrisy, be gone your foolish days.

Enter thee oh harmony, enter thee oh spirit of heart
Fill me now with thine wisdoms voice, that true balance may return.

No longer, broken shards of ice, nor mist, nor fog, nor tears.
for life shall blossom within this soul, as pure essence upon chariots fly.
Non-beyond shall ever harm, nor, future lies be told.
Hearken now broken soul, be banished evermore.

Of word that was given, there were but two………

I am mine own being

………. one leading to the path of light,
…the other of; damnations tongue,
I curse thee, and I send thee, far into the night, to be ever consumed, in the darkest hour. Ever diminished, unto nought, I refuse thee passage of ever return, I blacken your forces so be gone now, my final word, be gone. Oh, thee of a liar's path

I rest me now.
Empty but true,
awaiting the essence of truth,
for as this desired truth shall arrive,
tis I, who shall stand and grow.
Now tis I who shall lead the way,
for strength and truth shall be,
and through this living fire shall from the ash's wisdom thrive
Onward now with spirit cleansed and awareness evolved within,
never more shall this being walk,
as death through the lips of the impure.

I seek to learn

To know,
Feel,
Endure,
Embrace.
I seek to love.
I long to live,
To know passion, warmth,
Natural balance.
I long for harmony
I await the call of the essence
The unbounded truth
The purity and purpose
Do I wait alone?
Do you seek also?
Is your soul restless? Your heart, empty?
Take my hand, together we shall step into
The core of spiritual bliss
Be not afraid
Allow the vibrancy of the natural world
envelope you're very being.

If this were the way

The Coordination of inspiration
The assigning of successful motivations
Facing all uncovered truths
The conceiving of awareness within the self
Having purposefulness of action, knowledge of ability
Verification of perception, maturity of wisdom
Far beyond the indoctrinations of false foundations
Powerful in self-confidence, disciplined decisions and honest determinations.
Challenging, intellectual ever cautious of foreboding avenues
Ever sensible.
Coherent, remaining purposeful, tactful and sincere.
Never forceful, always flexible,
Compassionate and sympathetic toward the perceptions of others
Living with persistence yet obliging and kind Stable in patience, calmness and generosity.
Overcoming selfish desires. Prudent, ethical and morally resourceful.
Effective and clear sighted, competent and always respectful of others.
Playful and adventurous, yet ever remaining, dependable, modest and polite.
Observant and encouraging, always seeking ways of achieving balanced performances

If only this were the way

Welcoming and considerate in all interactions
Ever aware, ever conscientious of, the humanistic needs of others.
Gathering and transferring valued nurture amongst all.
Ever ready to learn, ever ready to move on with pure harmony and gratefulness
Engulfing your very soul and the hearts of others without selfish desire
Were this the way of things, were this the way of being, universal, without conceit
I for one would bow before the unknown, in gratitude for, the wonders of creation.

In a moment of thought

In moments of thought
Where in dreams I am caught
Through shadows of fear I walk
Alone
Through the passage of time
This journey of mine
Leaves me longing for a child's lost home
Oh, essential life
Oh, essence of birth
Gathering of wisdom
Finding self-worth
Leave me not to squander my life in greed
Allow me from foolishness and folly be freed.

Indoctrinations and fallacies

Mind be still, if but for a moment.
Give me peace, that I can be at one with myself.
Allow me peace, that I may have choice,
One moment with god, is all that I ask.
My god, my choice of god, my need of god, my pure god, the god of no name
the god of that which is, the god I do not know, the outer, the inner,
the beginning the end.
The creation, the before and the after, the seed, the essence, the purity of life.
That of my blood, my heart, my soul, that which is in every breath,
Yet you oh devils mind. who confuses and destructs, with your many barbarous way's.
It is you who are the cause of; my unpleasing actions, you truly are the bane of my existence.
I shall fight you.
I need but, the slightest glimmer of light to shine through your darkness
That I can step beyond the shadows that you cast. 'Tis in this single moment that I shall find *the* god that I seek, the spirit of life, the joy of being, the purity of nature's own course.
Yet even though I know not of its name, nor form, nor gender, I feel the veil of pure spirit is ever there waiting.
It is in all I see, and all I hear.
It is in the brightness of the sun, of the moon and endless stars. It is in the waters and very earth upon which I dwell. It is in the very call of; all-natural life.
It is the essence of; so much yet unknown.
Yet, what of, they? Indoctrinated with the fallacies of; dreamers and false prophets.
You heed the word of all, storing their stories. hoarding the gossips and meanderings of mere mortal tongues.
Yet what purpose when truth is of so little content, what need of this encyclopaedic nonsense?
For the very seed that is sought, is buried so deep beneath the mountain of make believe, hidden from human heart.
Be rid of the rubble of mis-conceptions
Let the damnations and fabrications fall back into the abyss of ignorance from whence they came.
Better we replenish the seed of life, abide in the light of time……

Indoctrinations and fallacies

……remaining no longer a prisoner
allowing the essence of existence to also be freed
lighting up the darkness, dispersing that of shadows and confusions, so that creation awaken once more, that harmony bring balance and peace.

If but my crazy journey mind, would take heed of me.
That it should join and work with me.
Then perhaps greater love and purpose shall ever be known.

In times of survival

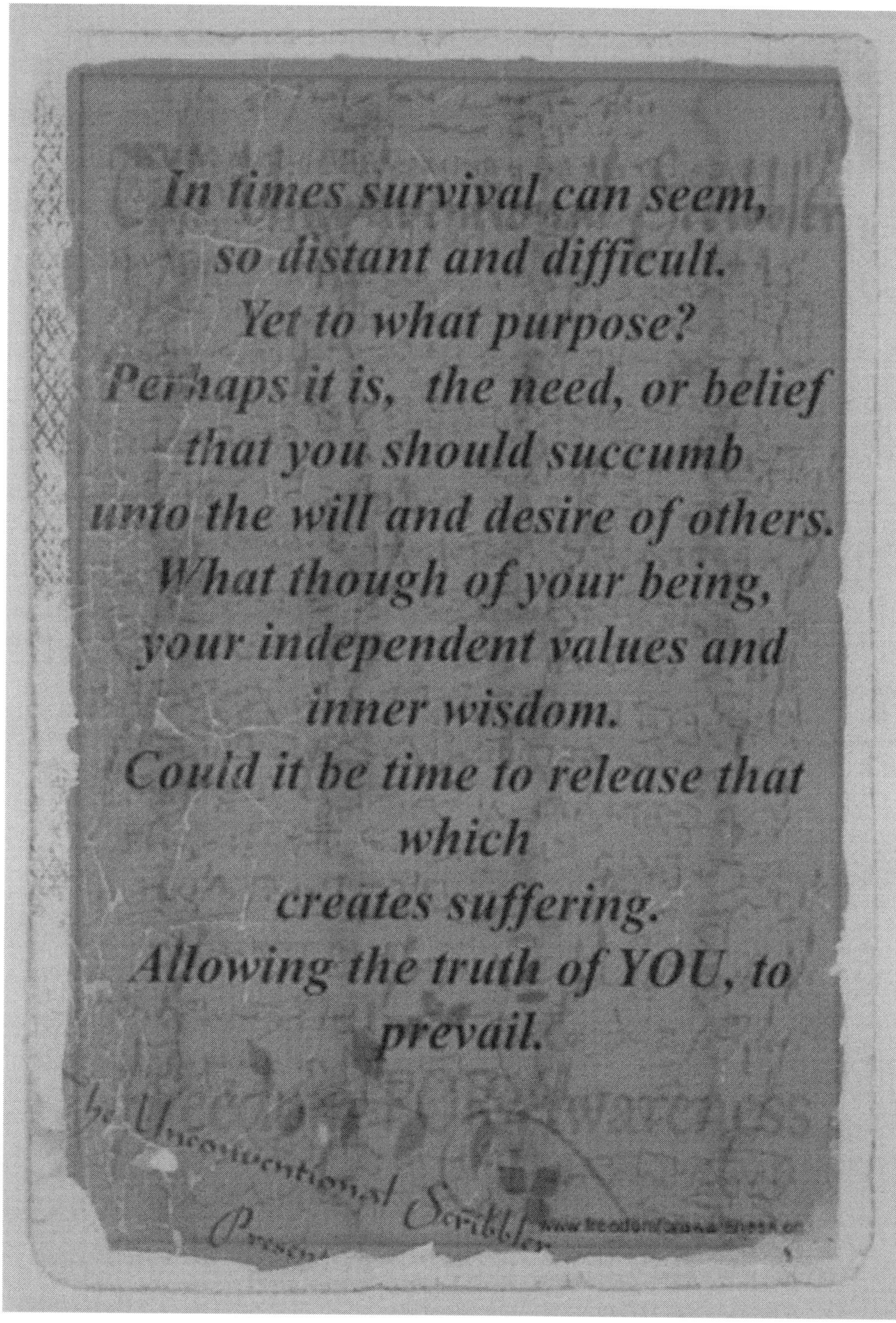

Information overload

Within this world of mine
Information overload how can this be.
For isn't life a gift of actual simplicity.
A bird a bird a fish a fish a pureness of creation.
Information overload did my parents know no better
When they led me into the beginnings?
Did teachers know no better when they told me
This is the truth of life.
Ever surrounded by information overload
Beliefs of misguidance, a thousand voices strong
Information overload.
What of personal truth, of experience.
Of life lived, of self-recognition
Of purpose, of self-value of personal being, in harmony with
The natural course of things. That which has not been altered through
Egos and so-called intelligence.
Information overload, unproven statements, labels
Mind blowing inaccuracies, consumerism and media produced distortions.
So, what of I, in this day, this moment
Information meltdown.
For if it is not of nature's proof
I have no desire toward the knowledge of lies.

Is there a place

If there is a place, then pray take me
Where no lies await, where tongues are true, and actions clear.
Where neither fear, nor exclusion exist and there is purpose for, every soul.
Let us not kill, nor hate, nor deceive.

What then? What if, we cared as one.
To empty the streets of the homeless, fill the bellies of the poor.
Awaken the value of our children, awaken wisdom and right to live,
A place where, blood is not shed, and homes are filled with love.
Where curses are that of the past, and laughter awakens with the sun.
Where word is truth and Man is man, Women, woman and nurture is but true nature of the child.
A place where each name is pure, where dreams are no longer sour
Where neither Adam, nor Eve, nor apple any longer take the blame.
Where, no more the sadness and sorrow thrive, or that of, corruption, or destruction of our natural world
A place where none stand idly by whilst conceit and cowardice curse the day
No longer the death of the morrow, with no spirit, nor soul, nor light of the eyes
Nor hope.......
Take me now, to the place where my body be covered, for I have failed as many shall fail
In the search for perfection
May new life be found, for perhaps life needs to grow anew,
with, the eradication of .... human ignorance.

Jigsaw mind

Of what is there to be sure of.
Tis this mind that turns and tumbles
A whirlpool of debris cast from the past and fragmented beyond recognition.
Nay, not a whirlpool. A tornado twisting and whining its way through mine own self.
Disrupting, disturbing, ripping apart all in its path.
I have to laugh, I am forlorn, however, I am neither blind, nor stupid
I am sane enough to know, this is not the true way of things.
I shall raise my hands and voice and loudly demand all to cease
All the rumblings, and the tumbling, and the fumbling, of this existence, that becomes more like…. a jigsaw, every day.
However, the pieces get smaller, with many notches and grooves
How am I to piece them together?
They change shape and colour; they do and undo themselves, skittering and scattering all around me
Yet how can this be, for, they are not without, they are within, contained, yet not maintained.
Yes, that is what I must do, I must maintain them.
My head is a jigsaw, it is a challenge of the truth, the way forward eureka..., eureka, at last, a piece here, that piece there.
Tick tock, tick tock, today I shall patiently begin.
Piece by piece, by piece by piece …… until, the tornadoes inside subside…...
……and the jigsaw becomes whole.

Last shadow

Hidden beneath a shadow,
such as none seen before.
This shadow had not the darkness of the past
For it radiated an illumination dancing around me as though it was if alive
Vibrant with life, powered by the very essence of time
an experience that was, mine alone.

The wonder was so strong I wanted only to share it,
in the hope that you may feel it also, or, be prepared for, the day,
your own final shadow shows itself.
How can I describe such feeling that purged through my being?
The colors, vibrations, fearful and yet of such peace.
As this wonder ate its way through each particle of my existence,
I felt growth as never before,
I could feel my body stretched far beyond any known space
Was this life. The air in my lungs became like that of the winds
My blood flowed like the oceans and streams
My heart pounding as the eruption of volcano's, my very essence fiery and wild
Such vibrancy as I flowed within and without all that were,
the sounds of a thousand orchestras drawing me ever closer
Closer, closer to what. How far could I travel? How much greater could I grow?
This surely was the journey of life beyond life.
Exhilarated I continued, unable to express the entity of I, for, I, had become, no more than, a past of ignorance.
Here before me danced wisdom to the sweetest sounds never heard.
Here was the very seed of a beginning, a birth far beyond all dreams.
Such harmony, blossoming of colors, fragrances pure and untainted
What was I before my memory fading, drifting far beyond the essence of now?
Born I am born, I am awakened unto my natures worth, I am alive in the essence of being.
No longer seen by mortal soul.

Let me take you by the hand

Let me take you by the hand, lead you through the streets of life
Where people suffer in mental pain, through false creators of, daily strife
Let me take you on a magic tour. come with me through the open door of;
mental madness and conspiracies, Indoctrinations and so-called therapies
Here you'll meet those who for their own, the powers that be who have overthrown
the way of compassion and sympathy, tis they who take our right to be.

Our suffering is like but food to them, they live and thrive on our mayhem,
to line their pockets with greed and pride, through the ways of sufferings which they supplied.
Throughout our life.

Just look around you feel the pain, of the nameless ones, named insane,
They who seek but to live and breathe, on this, god's earth, oh how he must grieve
As he sees the people who are led to drown, by they who have trodden down,
the law of life.
Yet through this open and magic door we stand amongst the sick and poor,
we hold the seed of god's right hand. and I am sure he must understand
It is they not us who have destroyed the truth, and surely one day beneath gods roof
We shall stand again, our heads held high, and they shall hear the peoples cry.
For, we are truth upon this earth and have been from our time of birth
and they who turned our minds astray shall surely come to rue the day
that they played God.

Life within thine self

Why is this, that we allow the self to be swallowed up by dreams and fantasies?
These desires, Infatuated by the addictions that lead nowhere but to disaster
But then, do not all addictions.
Is this not like all other sufferance, always seeking, that which cannot be had
inner suffering caused to mind and body.
how foolish the delusions in so many manners
Jokers of life, self-foolish ones be true
Face yourself for the mockery you lay at your own feet
Judge yourself be honest in your words
For you know the wrongs you commit against yourself
You fight as though an envious brother or sister against yourself
Envious and greedy of self-Unknowing of; your own mind.
one minute to the next, torment and loneliness raining upon your own head
In ignorance and false pride you stand, your ego ripping at your very soul
your own shadow laughing in your face.
When will you awaken? See the folly of foolish ways.
When will you on bended knees, see yourself for the traitor that you are
Lies, like flies, multiplying creating black clouds within your own dreams
Not one day of honor do you live unto yourself?
Blind conceited and foolish the dance of devils your daily right

How long this song of lament, until the Awakening
The opening of eyes, of the heart, spirit, and soul.
awakening this being that has lain forever dormant
no longer to suffer and blame, to cheat and cry
see the emptiness that surrounds you

Yet how would it be, if you were to awaken anew,
afresh with new found knowledge.
For we are more than just shadows
we are not fools, we can be wise
we are the heart of life if we would but listen to, the wisdom within
that which begs us to step out of this darkness in which we shroud ourselves.
Throw down the cross
Release yourself from the thorns
And live, yes live as a natural being
Live as nature would live
Live as truth would live
Living shall bring harmony, balance and contentment to your being
the earth is not far from you awaiting your space to fill………

Life within thine self

……………………Remorse after death would be a sad thing, such unrest for eternity
So, awaken now even there may be death the morrow
Least be but for one day
One hour true to thine own being
With neither hurt nor harm to another
distance yourself from the darkness of self-pity and sorrow
see the warmth and pureness of your life's blood
as it pulsates through your living body
fully alive, in body, In heart, In mind, in soul, the spirit of true existence,
Now is the time to welcome yourself, with open arms.

Lost time

A story of lost time. Of life lost. A heavens angel tale
Unknown to man for it is not his time.
This is a world of before, a time of this and that, how all combined, to create another.
A time when existence existed, nurtured by day and by night.
No words, just being. No opposite, for there was no need, there was just it, and us, part of an angel's lore, simple watchers over time.
No form had we, only a mighty force to preserve that of natural balance.
Whisperers upon the winds, gatherers of fallen ones, protectors of disease
not all was grand, no paradise, just an existence, as was.

How was it so. Who knows? for it was not our place to question, and for those who did,
there was a vanishing, a forgotten space in time.
Amid the eruptions and disruptions of land and sea, as the earth buckled, stretched and yawned, resting itself, in a peaceful void of harmony infusing with all around.
Such powers rained upon this earth, a growth soon far beyond an angel's task.

And hence was formed earth, creation, abundance of life to nurture
alas though we could not foresee, the imbalance within our seed.
To begin, there was harmony, much rejoice, as creatures cared and valued, was one with all,
And then…
How can we know when it occurred, when one smote another?
Yet high in the heavens, the balance turned, dis-harmony spread like fire
Where once waters had run pure, blood flowed, and they who were to be shepherds, became destroyers of the land.
The earth shuddered and tried to heal. To rid itself of this disease
yet no eruption, nor flood of oceans, could eradicate this poisonous source.

Tis true amongst these sickened creatures, there were they who tried to right the wrongs,
However, they of darkness became power, creating power laws, with laws of death, and fear, and hell became the domain on earth.
We the watchers were held by nature with no powers to alter course
With intervention, came perilous cost, for to close and we would also fall,
becoming as one tainted, upon this earth.
However, for love of this natural world, thousands upon thousands came upon all lands and shores……

…. So soon their powers diminished, lights of grace failed them, for the poison was so far spread……..

Lost time

………Few of us remained, spread wide and far apart, watching the destruction grow
Yet what can we do but perish ourselves amid the throes of death
Now and then one of us will tempt to intervene, but the greed of mankind runs far too deep
Fear not though yea of hope, for never shall we dessert this earth,
oh, natural beauty fair, the time shall come when the poisonous beast shall be over thrown
that harmony and balance shall flow once more.

Life in the beginning

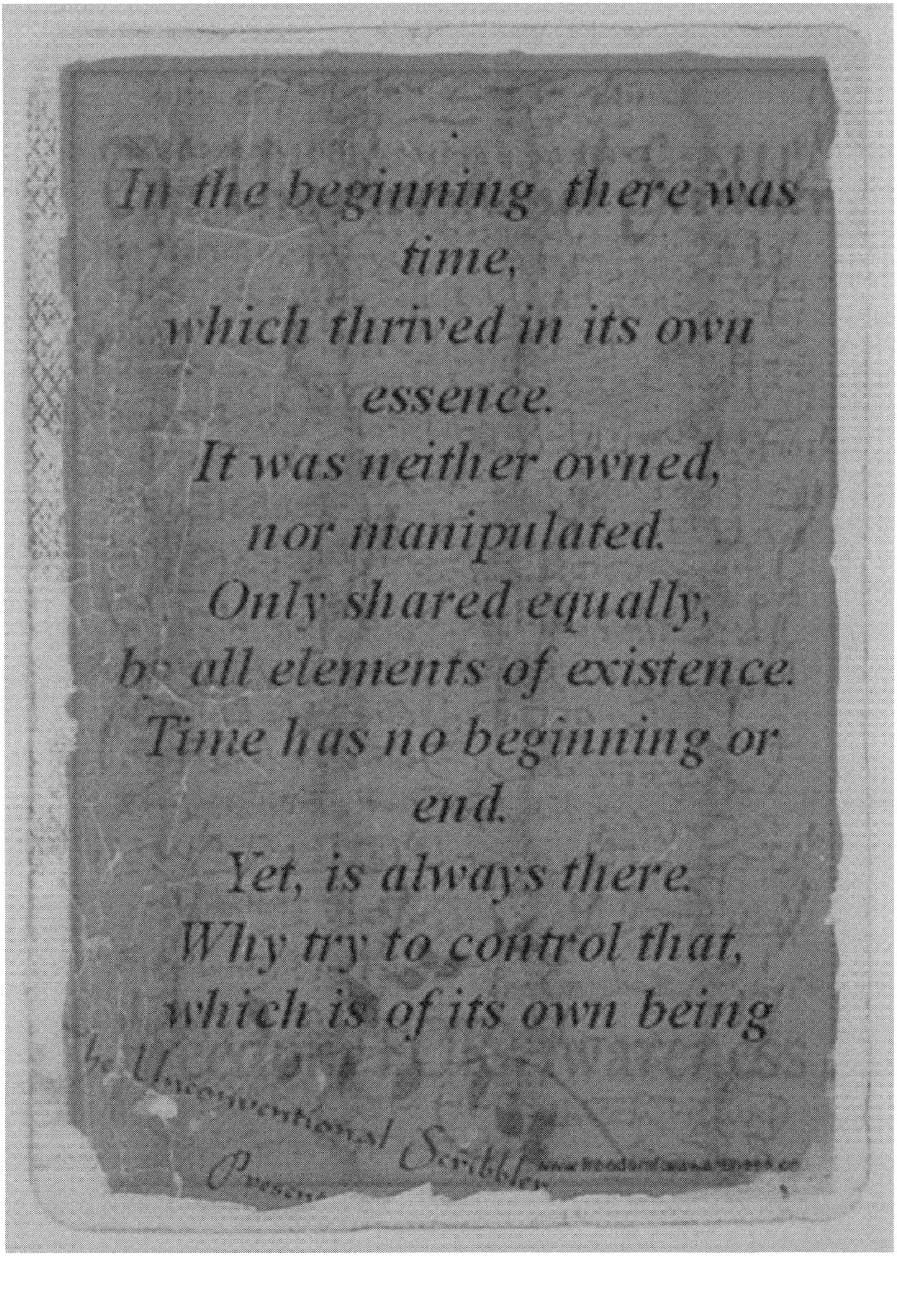

Lucky

I am lucky to have what I have
No, I am not lucky I am blessed
No, blessed is not right either
I am in the correct connection
It is important that I neither get conceited or complacent
It is important that I recognize the inner truth
That which is the essence of life has become brighter in my life
It is that brightness that I should continue to value
Ever in gratitude and appreciation
To love and to accept the wonders of existence
To ever be aware of balance and imbalance
It is for me to daily care for all,
To be aware of others
To abide by the way of love compassion and regard
May it be that I remain ever in awe of that which is
May it be that I always return as I receive?
May I remain ever grateful?
And offer my thanks as well as thanks to myself
for the accepting of the truth within.
May I ever be willing to learn and to listen?
And may this contentment lead me toward
helping others to find contentment also.

Praise to that which is.

Magic

To thee oh unknown
Who or what is this that I seek
What form or magic do I imagine?
I am persuaded of, that something outside of natural awareness perhaps of miracles
I seek that of synchronicity, ritual, the key word, that mine prayers shall be of value

To desire without effort becomes pointless
What point of wishing
Knowing nought of other world laws
One will never grow an oak tree by planting a sycamore seed
So, it is because of many variables that magic becomes.
.
Acceptance and release of the past, permission to move on and achieve
Discovering and knowing what is available to ones needs
Being aware that there are limitations and the knowing of them.
To be motivated, through the excellence of the unknown
Yet not out of competitions nor greed,
Simply a path toward the achievement of natural bent.

I therefore, am persuaded of, that something outside of mortal awareness.
Perhaps it is of miracles.
I seek that of synchronicity, ritual. The key which unlocks.
May it be that mine prayers shall be of value,
that mine desires are of harmless intent.
That the magic of life,
become the ruling of mine presence.

Manipulation

A game of manipulation, of torment and simple life dissatisfaction.
For should truth be discovered, mankind may well feed itself to the earth.
The one creature that has lost all place and reason, a creature that believes itself beyond reproach.
We the hunters of disharmony
We the hunters of war, famine, poverty and the earned right of shame
Yes shame, shame of our being, never satisfied, always looking to alter that of originality
Not satisfied with being, ever wanting to be, other than.
No essential connection, nor, place within earth's great span.
Nothing natural about this human species, other that it lives and dies,
What then have we have searched for so long? The perfect race, the perfect being.
Create laws outside of nature's law, only to break them, for greed and that of vanity.

So simple life should be, yet so sad it is
The many fools fashioned by others,
The weakness of the unknowing, the separation from dreams,
such beings creating the imbalance of its own existence.
Lost with little wisdom can only look upon the devastation.
Lies upon lies. Deception and manipulation, throughout a world given for nurture and harvest
Such sadness and empty souls, the knowing that there is a truth, yet ever so far from it.

Words that are unutterable yet lay dormant the world over.
We know, we know that we are liars, deceivers and the like
We know that we are parasites and makers of doom
We know that we have walked far beyond the boundaries of freedom
We have chosen our course against the way of things; therefore, suffering is duly ours.
Nod not your head in agreement, nor shake it in disapproval, for, until there is the desire to be part of, none other than hypocrisy shall there be……

……. Who am I to breach the silence.
I am as you, by whatever code you live.
Suffering in the same grandiose life……….

Manipulation

……….I am no more, nor less.
I too am a liar, a fraud, a coward, an inventor of ignorance and vanity.
I too will lie and die for surrender unto peace. for harmony within this species, of which I am a part.
For yourself and only through yourself, can you know the path of your own destruction or beatitude.
Is there a good word to say?
Is there wisdom to impart?
Wouldn't that be such folly?
When so many have lied before.

Many hours do we spend

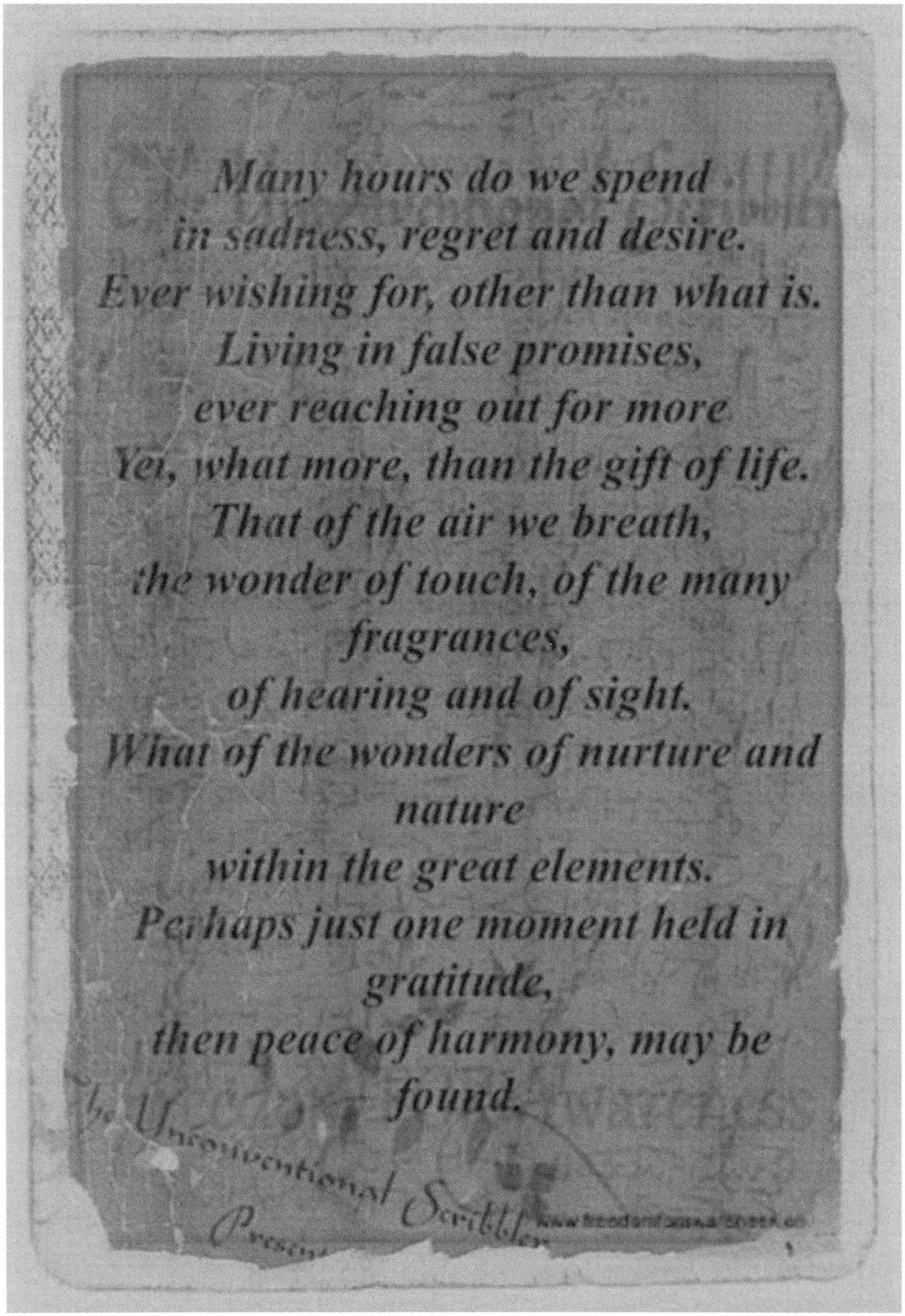
Many hours do we spend
in sadness, regret and desire.
Ever wishing for, other than what is.
Living in false promises,
ever reaching out for more
Yet, what more, than the gift of life.
That of the air we breath,
the wonder of touch, of the many fragrances,
of hearing and of sight.
What of the wonders of nurture and nature
within the great elements.
Perhaps just one moment held in gratitude,
then peace of harmony, may be found.

by Unconventional Scribbler

Mind, soul, spirit

Swallowed up by fantasies?
Infatuated by addiction
the seeking after that which is not to be
what inner suffering caused to that of mind and body
What foolish delusions, such jokers of life
what mockery we lay at our feet.
Judge yourself, be honest in your words
For we each know the negatives easily committed against the self.

The fight against shadows, as though envious of our own being
Unknowing of the mind from one minute to the next
Torment and loneliness raining down upon desired visions

creating ignorance and false pride with ego ripping at the very soul
that shadow of self, voicing distant words.
"When will you awaken? can you not see the folly of your ways,
when will you, on bended knees, see yourself for the traitor that you are
creating lies, like flies, multiplying, creating black clouds within dreams.
Not one day of honor do you give yourself?
Blind conceited and foolish you allow the dance of devils be your daily plight
How long fool, how long this song of lament
Awaken fool to your trickery
The mirages you create with childish gloom.

Fool oh fool waken

Open your eyes, your heart, your spirit, your soul.
awaken this being that lays forever dormant
How you suffer and blame. How you cheat and cry
How you look at the emptiness that surrounds you
hidden safely within a world of non-satisfaction
A deceiver, a narcissist, rotting in false desires
yet how would it be if you were to Awaken anew,

afresh with new gained knowledge
For you are more than just a shadow. You are more than just a fool,
You are wise for the years have taught you the heart of life
therefore listen to your true wisdom within
for it begs you to step out of the darkness in which you shroud yourself..........

……………Throw down the cross, release yourself from the thorns
allow yourself to live as a natural being
Live as nature would live, Live as truth would live. Live as a creature of compassion, of kindness and acceptance of the pure you
Living shall bring harmony and balance and contentment to your being
Awaken fool for the earth is not far from you
awaiting your space to fill
Remorse after death will change naught of any suffering
So awaken now even if you must die the morrow
Least be but for one day, true to thine own being, With neither hurt nor harm to another.

Distance yourself from the darkness of self-pity, see the warmth and pureness of your life's blood
as it pulsates through your living body, tis now the time to welcome yourself with open arms.

Minds own truth

Being honest with one's self, no easy task
For many outside influences block the path of clarity
The wants and needs of others
The politics of world and region
The ever-growing powers of commerce.
The ever diminishing of self-value and worth.
However, though not an easy task
we all have the availability of, choice to change.
Personal identity and self-awareness can create contentment,
as can gratitude and the recognition of one's own given abilities.

Finding Ways forward. Not such an easy task
Why.? For that of the mind, because of infused attachment.
Through fear, of loss, of gain, perhaps because of, complacency.
Whichever cause can only be known, or rather, discovered by the self.
That, the conclusion shall come easily is ever of doubt
for the outcome can never be truthfully predicted.

How though to rectify that which has already passed?
How to alter that which has already been?
Yet how could this be
For it is only in an immediate moment of time that change can save grace.
'Tis in self only, not of others that can make the difference in the now.
Only through determination, desire and actions,
can come the understanding, purpose and value of being
'Tis in self only, that the moment one lives in, is of either harmony or chaos
the choice comes only from self within.
As for the errors of others, this is not of concern
For each individual needs to correct their own self without judgement upon others.
There are times when emotions become far greater than truth,
therefore, delusions soon overcome the purest of thoughts.
Negativity shall ever affect one's moment, through choice and lack of awareness.

Perhaps the answer is in stillness, evaluating actions, thoughts and purpose,
To truly discover that of contentment and peace within the self.
only answers, sought deeply within shall bring unto each,
a path, leading the way of discovery toward the purest of nature's course.
There can only ever be the being and the passing of self-recognition,
none other is responsible for the happenings and outcomes,
other than that, of, one's own being, responding to; nature's essence.
Discovering, the knowing of, one's own minds truth.

Minds world

Tis the mindset that builds a desperate need of attention
Yet what it can achieve is limitless,
with a correct way of thinking.
Life is given, and one day shall be done
therefore, time offers all a chance.
Sadly, it is through choice,
that of lost opportune.
creating blame and guilt upon the self.
The past is the past, yet what of the present and future.
Faith can guide the move forward
Releasing the pitying of self
One cannot remain responsible for the happiness of others
For it is upon each to discover responsibility for self.
Not to hide behind fruitless repetitions of the day before.
Each moment in time is precious, how much wiser to utilize it.
Discover and be content
Make your world as you wish it to be
For today is your beginning,
grasp it or lose it,
choice ever remains that of;… each individual.

Natural wisdom

The essence of natural wisdom
Tis mine own self, that darkened, the given path
Tis none but ignorance, that cast me, far from wisdoms word.
Tis now, none but foolishness, that I sorrow over wasted years.
there is only but now, to bring mine self-unto, the harmonies
of nature's gift.

What is there more than, the true essence of being?
What more than the value of each breath?
What more than discovering the pureness of existence.

For all is no more than state of mind.
Of blindness toward that of inner wisdom.
All is no more than, fear of, that which is essential truth.

Tis in sadness that I recognize the futility of mine own species.
Ever seeking that which is already within.
the value of each individual's connection to, the spirit of nature way.

Yet it is not for me to investigate the way of others,
nor to judge, condemn, nor teach,
for each is unto their own of, acceptance.
The path of balance, of chaos, or, that of darkness.

Yet it is for me to know mine own freedom.
For, 'tis mine choice alone as to the making of time.

Nature knows

Nature knows, glows, offers the solution

Since that of evolution

Creativity has always awaited that moment

When the soul meets the soul

And the heart becomes free

So here now is one of those moments

A time of sharing, caring and creative involvement.

Tis a sadness that life can incur negativity

A sadness that many suffer from instability.

Yet life is, as life is, and always offers choice

To share our creativity through our actions and voice.

Natures breast

If one can become one within nature's breast
Embodied with life and full of zest
Can turn away from mankind's hold
Stay true to self and ever bold
If one could awaken and be aware
In acceptance that nature is always fair.
That harmony and balance shall ever prevail
ever in the wake of chaos's trail.
To trust, have faith, to act in accord
Is a given right, we each, can afford.

Natures breath

When physical love has abandoned you
and darkness veils your path
seek beyond the stars
where your true soul awaits your call.
For love awaits you in the forests,
as beneath the ocean's waves.
upon each beam sent by the sun
to spread in harmony.
All of this is within your palm
reach out, release, let go
breathe in the pureness of nature's breath
amid the golden glades.
tis here sweet soul in timeless time
that our aura shall become as rainbows
a guiding path for others.

Natures gift

I find myself in a whirlpool of shadows
seeking but one single rose with the fragrance of eternal life.
each rising morn, I reach out to that which is not there.
I feel the thorns of the past ripping through my skin
piercing my heart choking me with un-flowered tendrils.
I grasp at life in its simplest form
never knowing the truth of truth.
I cry out in screams of silent torment
I pray for the garden to flourish.
I awaken breathless to the air of the living.
I place my feet upon the awaiting earth.
I feel the fire of passion and desire flood through me
as the waters recede leaving me upon shores I do not know.
here I languish with naught but empty horizons,
all this for the sake of a rose,
a truth beyond truth a value,
a purpose a meaning to be captivated and shared
yet I find myself in a whirlpool of shadows where the rose is but a dream.
Until I walk in Harmony with the balance of nature's gift.

Natures quest

Hope and happiness, the desire to discover,
wisdom of light, elements of, universal truth.

Seeking freedom for awareness, of self and its means
rejecting indoctrinations. Becoming one's own soul.
The search for; fulfilment, overshadowed by desires.
The need to Step back, from clouded thoughts.

Breathe in that of nature's gift
With neither that of judgement, nor, expectation.

Hearken unto that, of your purest being
do not fear that of emptiness,
for it is within that very emptiness, that truth, shall prevail.
Release yourself from the minds of others,
Least they Create that of many misgivings.

Allow yourself freedom, without fear of loss
For, though there be many forms of deception,
Nature shall ever support and guide you.

Allow your pure essence to become your chariot.
Allow yourself, to taste, to feel, to smell,
to have great vision of; that which is pure in all directions.
That which gives life through birth and re-birth in so many ways.

Listen, but be ever aware of tales and stories,
beware of false instructions,
of another being's perception and experience.

Balance yourself in harmony expecting nothing,
yet receive all that is given, in gratitude,
for these things come as a gift from a universe unknown.
Therefore, treasure each breath, and acknowledge each experience.

Allow the way of inner truth to lead you, even though there may be moments of
insecurity,
for it is only through, that of chaos and balance,
that harmony arises.

Nature's way

Within the life of they who seek, not they so easily led
Who bleed within their own life, not of another who has bled.
of they who strive through sufferance, needing no cross to bare
For it is these the souls of purest heart, ne'r as tainted as they who swear,
their oaths unto that unproven, creating myths from ancient tales
they who insist their prophecies shall balance out the scales.
Yet turn to truth of centuries, rising sun and seasons sure
Offering none but golden harvest for they who e'er endure.
They who know true balance, who live to grace the day.
Never seeking more than harmony, to freely pave the way,
for the future generations, that they too respect the land
with neither guilt, nor false wisdoms. Of dealings underhand.
But Pure truth and kindred spirit, for family hearth and home.
free from that of dogmas, mankind standing for their own.
The times of lies and slavery of false doctrines have outlived their day
As have they who preach words of poison, destroying that of nature's way

No feeling, no mind

Not knowing nor being
No feeling, no mind
No reason, just another mission,
a transition
A decision.
The making of moments.
Turn around, walk around
Pick up the pieces
Don't fight your way out
Hide in the shadows
Beware, believe, take care
The sun rises soon
Your value is a wonder
Your voice is like thunder
Yet you shake like a child
In a wilderness without rainbows.
Not knowing nor being
No feeling no mind

No Judgement

Perhaps there are times when, change is a word that is meaningless
when the words of self-responsibility are futile
And words like wellbeing, good life, happiness and freedom of choice are just like passing whispers in the wind.

For the survivors of wrong choices, continuously striving to discover better living. The daily discovery of endless life change concepts
each one brilliant for whoever wrote or conceived the idea for themselves, that is.
It is amazing how many people have the easy answer to another person's life professing that to do just as they say will help you discover the great miracle of living.

The hard and simple fact of life is, that you are your own healer
Your own friend and enemy. You will either listen to yourself, or, you will not
The choice and responsibility ever remain with you, for there is no saviour, other than that of your own soul.
What point then is there to this article, perhaps absolutely none because I alone travel my journey of self-discovery, as you on yours.
We are not at the same place, at the same time,
nor have we experienced emotions alike.
Maybe though. as we pass each other on our journey we can recognise that our suffering is shared by many. Tis at this time both compassion and empathy can be given and received, without judgement.

No-one else

Never being, never knowing, nor understanding.
Never seeing, nor hearing, ever blind to.
Wishing, desiring, craving. Gaining, losing.
Tis many times sad, but true.
Holding onto, grasping for more
Dreaming of, planning for, adapting to.
Fighting against, hiding from, delusional mind.
Indifferent, afraid, tormented by time
Broken as a jigsaw, alone with the devil
Lack of fulfilment, no motivation, internal mayhem
Dark skies, dark days, dark nights. Dark dreams.
Pretending, intending, demanding of visions.
Wanting of clarity, in need of pure love.
The seeking of reward, for a life so far unlived.
The turning of fortune, the awareness of existence.
Therefore, comes time for self, the opening of heart
Awakening to the becoming of the sweetness of life
As one's self, in truth, in harmony with perfection
Unto you, the wonders, of all that is.
Tis ever your world to choose, it cannot be that of another.
All love flowing toward growth of self-love for that of self
And no-one else.

No reason

With no reasoning that I could understand
I stood before a barren land
Yet all before me flourished fine
That which was barren was of my mind

Nature's perfumes in all surround
The perfect textures of growth and ground
Yet here was I, lost to Gaia's voice
Alone in bleakness, a shadows choice

Neither sun, nor breeze, nor bird in flight
To penetrate this, my saddened plight.
Yet from a corner deep within the soul
A voice whispered release, do not control

I listened, inhaled the pureness of breath
Stepping out from the darkened death
Life within me began to grow
and Nature's surround began to glow.

No sorrow

No feeling, no meaning, no sense of self
No desires or ambition, no care for great wealth
No feelings of wonder nor pleasure or worth
No visions nor awareness nor purpose of birth
No moment of pleasure for spirit or heart
No thoughts for a future nor a wish to take part
No meaning, no purpose no value nor gain
No emotions of love, of envy, or shame
Empty, forlorn, adrift in a void
A life time of sadness, no pleasures enjoyed
Sorrowful, sorrowful perhaps this is true
Yet you know not me, as I know not you
We are but shadows, in a play we pretend
To be happy and joyful right to the end
Oblivious to our actions, oblivious to truth
Oblivious of life's meaning, of which there's no proof.

Sorrowful, sorrowful such a tale of man's woe
And yet I am contented in this sadness I know
I seek no deliverance, nor forgiveness of sins
For admittance of defeat is where it begins
The search of great power, of envy and greed
Of the exotic desire for things we don't need.

Oh sorrowful. Sorrowful this heart of lost time
Sorrowful, sorrowful, this sad tale of mine.
Yet I am now free from the curses and lies
Of the pain and the suffering one always denies

Freed from dreaming for what is not true
No longer false fantasies, of paradise, ensue
No longer encapsulated by deceit or desire
Or under the illusion of the need to admire

I am me, I am free, and yet still I concern
For the indoctrinated ones, who never shall learn.
However, who am I, to speak of life's fate?
I am the nightmare, from which we don't awake.

Of that with which we are born

The soul of creativity in all its forms

The value of, each, individual's creation

The wonder of the spirit

The inspiration, motivation, inclusion

The escape from delusion

That steals from the heart

Causes distress in but a moment

Devaluing the originality

Taking away the essence

Of that which we were born with.

Nature knows, glows, offers the solution

Since that of evolution

Creativity has always awaited the moment

When the soul meets the soul

And the heart becomes free

So here now is one of those moments

A time of sharing, caring and creative involvement.

Tis a sadness that life can incur negativity

A sadness that many suffer from instability.

Yet life is as life is yet offers us choice

To share our creativity through actions and voice.

Oh, to live

Oh, to live
Not but to cry
For life is of love and wonders sought
If only I could but search within
Open the door of truth
Awaken,
Become,
Realise.
Be grateful for the wonder of existence
For nature has given me a place
The universe and all within, have opened to me.
The secrets are no secret
They are an awakening showing splendour and amazement
Oh, love of life empty me of self-suffering
Allow me the right of wisdom that I may be grateful for this day
When yet again the elements and all that is
Allows me one more time to breathe in
the glorious breath of life.

Opportunity

The opportunity, the power of being in, creativities embrace.
The welcoming of pure soul, freeing itself from indoctrinated values.
The spiritual involvement, as if one with the universe.
What could there be greater than this.
The awakening of self, beyond
The soul of creativity in all its forms
The value of each, individual's creation
The wonder of the spirit
The inspiration, motivation, inclusion
The escape from delusion
That steals from the heart
Causes distress in but a moment
Devaluing the originality
Taking away the essence
Of that which we were born with.

Nature knows, glows, offers the solution
Since that of evolution
Creativity has always awaited the moment
When the soul meets the soul
And the heart becomes free
So here now is one of those moments
A time of sharing, caring and creative involvement.
Tis a sadness that life can incur negativity
A sadness that many suffer from instability.
Yet life is as life is yet offers us choice
To share our creativity through actions and voice.

Passion of life

Oh, passion of life I seek thee, wonders so far beyond
For all my mortal thought of paradise, in solitude must I remain.
Oh, wonders beyond shadows, hidden face, where lies your hidden warmth
though ever in my heart have I deeply searched.
Only ice and fear within evolves
Yet ever I hear your whisper clear, This I follow with passionate mind
Yet ever you elude me, I am forever that step behind.
Oh, season of such sweet embrace, though I ever seek your forgiving eyes
Nought but a veil of silk I see, Showing no script for destiny.
Ney purity can never be, for time has passed me by
Alas the future grows ever dimmer now,
leaving neither love, nor truth, nor gain.
Even though from dreams of loss, I awaken unto life's sweet promise
You my love who haunts me so, once again whisked away in flames
With saddened heart I walk the day, no shadow by my side
for there is no love can link my arm, for She is far beyond all prayers.
And yet somewhere must await my sweet embrace, a queen to be so adored
Yet I must remain torn of heart and mind, In a loneliness long endured,

Long gone now my soul regrets
this my spirit sobs and cries
oh, wait for me sweet tender love
Lest the passion truly dies.

Peace and harmony.

Within peace and harmony.
With gladness of heart.
Do I place myself with in your absence?
As daybreak's or as night falls.
The elements flourish.
Tell me.
of what greater value can I find but this.
For there is none above natures course.
My call is silent.
Least I disturb such peace.
I am filled with glory from each living entity
I place myself naked upon the earth.
My heart beats as does hers
I feel the song she sings.
The sun's rays dance, the Ambiance way.
In sweet chorus? I reach out to the heavens.

I am within natures Dance?
May blessings be.
In each part of each precious moment
Then so be it.
Through broken moods. Confusing times
crossing over hidden lines
trapped in spaces of soundless rooms
farfetched fantasies soon consume.
groundless meanings. No chartered course
lost vision of purpose within life's force.
In harmony of nature basic originality of time
true essence of meaning ever be mine
of fortunes nor riches do I seek for mine own
but wisdom and balance in great light be shown
tis ever and always that of divine grace
that can save the dark follies of our human race,

Perceptions

Perhaps it is the loneliness desired
A way of life, with the pleasure of self-ignorance
For even though there may a direction to go
There can be no ending,
For the mind chooses another thought
Leading to another path
Where present, past and future become entwined
Creating a world of which there is little knowledge
Perceptions become confused
Ever caught in the trap of the many, mindless indoctrinations.
How we know who another person is?
Of their need, their want their desire

For we see no more than a body
with shadowed eyes
knowing neither them nor their suffering.
Tis a truth for them only, their journey alone
Not of mine nor mine mind

Though I look vainly into the hearts of many
I realize there is only one person I need to investigate.
That of my very own soul
I alone am he, who creates disharmony and imbalance
It is I alone who chooses chaos
Mine wisdom and mine journey can be of peace and harmony
Maybe in this life
Yet never through the way of fallible others.

Perhaps despair

Prevention of disappointment
contentment of actuality in time
no less for no gain other than is
nourished and sheltered as need be
not governed by another's greed
satisfaction in the treasure of wellbeing
no fear nor desire to rule
why await the day of sorrow?
why live by the hand of ignorance?
be as one with all of nature's law
abide within the purest soul.

perhaps it is disappointment that haunts this being
perhaps it is self-loathing, perhaps it is loss of soul
or perhaps the lack of loves embraces.

This being, amid a world of unknowing others
what foolish notions torment the mind, leaving me in wanton despair
surrounded by invalid concepts, invented for power.
What power is there greater than, that which we do not know
this game of hate and blame is not even worthy of that we call hell.

Create, remake, alter the mistake, embrace one's self with love not hate
question, reason converse with self, suffering caused through greed for wealth
is there to be no relaxation through lack of satisfaction
in each way one may turn.

Fire raging through the soul, with no control of; the rage and anger
the dissatisfaction of the hand you were dealt
blame, anguish, sorrow, today and tomorrow.
Is that how it must be, or, can you find the consistency to remould, revalue
the indoctrinated mind.

oh yes indoctrinated, tricked, led, bled
not nurtured or empowered with the essence of worth
but incapacitated from your very becoming
I have no wish to remain this way……….

Perhaps despair

………I shall though have my day,
I shall walk away from the mumbo jumbo of speculation and false teachings.
Ignorance shall not infiltrate this being,
for this being looks into the natural way of things
the structure and the nurture of all other life forms.

Yet what an abomination we have allowed ourselves to become
what reality is left now we have been embedded with emotional despair.

This is not a love poem, nor guide, nor written truth
this is not the words of a sage, or of one wiser than another
this is but a reflection into each living soul.

Phenomena

There is no sense of time nor reason
for that which I should concern myself.
Nor of; injustice, nor pain, nor laughter.
Nor that of; Sadness, happiness, nor, wealth.

What then is there that gives purpose
to this essence of which I am.
How many questions?
Why search, what is there to gain,
Other than, endlessly sorting through shadows that have no meaning.
Who are you I wonder, other than a being, other than I.
What commonality do we hold?
Are our paths entwined?
Do I still breathe, if you do not exist?
Will you evaporate, should my life force be extinguished.

Why then do we fret so, over this and that
and the many endless complication of things,
which of course we somehow create.
What of this space in which I exist,
I know only of that which is mine, not yours,
nor theirs, nor another's,
'tis surely a bubble in which, I, me, exists.

Yet surely there is reason.
What of the many skills that a being gain?
Why have them if there is no reason?
What makes me, me, and, you, you?
What separates us one from another.

Phenomena.   A repetition of past events.
Cause and effect, or, effect and cause.
What matter.
For one piece of knowledge is made up of a thousand parts.
How much can I truly have the answer to?
When I speak of answer, do I mean truth,
What truth is this?
Who's truth?
For even truth has many guises,
owned by many, yet ever altered
throughout spans of time.

Prevention of disappointment

Contentment of actuality, in time
no less for no gain, other than is
nourished and sheltered as need be
not governed by another's greed
satisfaction in the treasure of wellbeing
no fear nor desire to rule
why await the day of sorrow?
why live by the hand of ignorance?
be as one with that of nature's law
abide within the purest soul.
perhaps it is disappointment that haunts this being
perhaps it is loss of soul, or, the lack of loves embraces
amid a world of unknowing others
what foolish notions torment the mind
creating states of wanton despair.
Surrounded by invalid concepts invented for power.
what power is there greater than that we do not know
this game of hate and blame is not even worthy of that we call hell.
Create remake alter the mistake
embrace one's self with love not hate
question, reason converse with self,
for suffering is caused through greed for wealth
no relaxation, no satisfaction
whichever direction one may turn
burn, burn, burn the fire raging through your soul, with no control
of the rage and anger and dissatisfaction of the hand you were dealt
blame, anguish, sorrow
today and tomorrow
is that how it has to be
or can you find the consistency, to remould, revalue
your indoctrinated mind
oh yes indoctrinated, tricked, led, bled
not nurtured or empowered with the essence of worth
but incapacitated from your very becoming
why remain this way, each should have their day………?

Prevention of disappointment

………….. walking away from the mumbo jumbo of speculation and false teachings.
Ignorance shall not infiltrate this being,
for this being looks into the natural way of things
the structure and the nurture of all other life forms.
What an abomination we have allowed ourselves to become?
What reality is left? now we have been embedded with emotional despair.
This is not a love poem, this is not a guide or written truth.
This is not the words of a sage, or, of, one wiser than another.
This is about final discoveries, awakening of days
……………...***I wonder how you shall see into yours.***

Pure essence of all that be

Oh, thine spirit, which is neither, of shape, of form, nor name.
How can I offer gratitude unto the unknown?
Awaken the seed within me that leads to thine way....
Oh thee of such splendor show me the truth of being.
That I to may flow in harmony and balance with thine nature

Pure Essence of all that be.

You are my path, you encapsulate all there is
through thine elements shall I live,
unto they shall I always turn my soul.
I am but as that below.
You are the earth upon the earth,
that which is beneath the oceans and within the skies,
as you are that which is far beyond the clouds.
How perfect this world and all that is given.
The seasons and natures quest,
Unto the sun, and the moon, I bow me down,
that I may be as one with 'the one'.
No judgement can be judged,
for all is within the all.
Grace me each day with your wonders
that true energies glow from within.

That awareness balance and harmony be unto all
So mote it be.

Pureness of essential self.

It has all been written before, the meaningless of material collection.

It has all been said before, the suffering that one creates in one's own life.

It has all been known before, the Karmic outcomes that are ever there, until that of realisation and awareness becomes an actuality.

Yet unto what can one turn to for alleviation from the pangs of guilt and remorse?

Where to be found, the actuality of a presence that forgives and releases the discomfort of mental anguish?

There are many who would readily, say,' take this path, or that'
for it shall set you free'.
Yet, I ask of myself are they too not in search of redemption, do they not also hide their true being, behind shadows of confusion. For surely any being that offers a pathway to freedom, seeking that of material return can have no true concept for; the way of things.

I ask of myself, is there such freedom that can wash away that which has been done............

.... It is with hardness of heart, that returns as mine answer, for truth is a great burden to bare.

There are they of, 'the collective' they who become of agreement to, 'this way or that'.

Yet how can they speak out, for are they not in judgement of another, when it is sanctuary from judgement that we all seek.

What then, or, where lies the purest truth, if all that passes have been before.

Why need I question that of mine own experience, if there is, none but repetitive despair.

Even though values may be of utmost importance, or that morals be a boundary in which to live. Still does judgement raises its head, for who can speak that which is deemed the truth.

What then of individual being, when all is stripped bare of instruction?

What then is there, that becomes the foundation for pureness of essential self.

Before me ever sits the true balance, of, not another's will, but, that of mine own...........

Pureness of essential self.

……. The answers of perfect collusion with 'that which is' where there are no bounds.

'Tis but in ignorance that I learned from the many who teach from their own learned ignorance.

'Tis but I who, in mental blindness and imbalance have created but delusions and degraded that of nature's path.

Yet to return unto the innocence of the unborn is not possible, until that of death, brings about the pure knowledge that contains the essence of truth.

Therefore, it seems that sufferance is but a continuum, a lesson carried within each being, leaving none that is unique unto the way, neither of this world nor that of any other.

I myself seek no more than truth of self, be it in, body, in mind, or of spirit.

Tis time and wisdom that shall teach me of other than, that of egos thirst.

Radiating Dreams

In the value of my dreams
I find mine own path to follow.
That of guiding light, of sounds supreme.
a gift given through the essence of the universe.
I turn to be as one, mine heart laid open to natures course.
In time I drift, finding myself far beyond the material world.
Enchanted within the powers that be, with no fear,
for I am as one in this essence of time.
'Tis here in the now that I breathe,
feel, touch and see the pureness of life's true being.
Gone are immature emotions,
the foolishness of negativity.
I welcome the knowledge and wisdom gifted by that which is.
May it be that the will of this instruction remain with me.
That my own essence radiates only that of contentment.

Rising

Even through the good times
We sooner recall the bad
forgetting times of laughter,
allowing in the sad?
Each day is different to each other
Offering ways to live our life
How can it be that it is easier?
To seek out ways of strife.
So, for today I shall make changes
And openly stand and face
The world and what it may offer
For the seeker to embrace.

I shall turn my back on the darker things
With courage and strength of heart
Tis with Humility and self-awareness
I shall gratefully play my part.
As to the how's the whys and when
We each know there shall be a choice.
So, for all the days that lay ahead
Give life a chance and so rejoice.

Self-assessment

I am not using the capabilities I have'
I have allowed myself to get caught up in negative thinking
I have allowed myself to become separated from the world
I have allowed myself to become full of remorse and self-pity
I have allowed myself to become confused and selfish
Only I can alter this situation by accepting my own personality
Only I can move forward by being honest in all my transactions and relationships
Only I can move forward positively through structuring myself

I allow my emotions to run my life
Unless I become aware of my own identity
I shall continue to live life without purpose or priority
Only I can change
Only I can recognize my purpose
Only I can enjoy the wonders of being alive
Only I and acceptance of, that which is, will bring me into the light.

Shadowed eyes

Perhaps, it is loneliness that I desire
A way of life, with the pleasure of self-ignorance
For even though there may a direction in which to go
There can be no ending as such,
For this mind chooses further thoughts
That leads to many another path, here present, past and future become entwined
Creating a world of which I have no knowledge.
Perceptions easily become confused
Ever caught in the trap of the many, and mindless indoctrinations.

How can I know the ways of another?
Of their need, their want, their desire

For I see no more than a body
That contains shadowed eyes and empty souls
I know neither them nor their suffering.
Tis a truth for them only, their journey alone
Not of mine, nor, mine mind

Though I look vainly into the hearts of many
I realize there is only one person I need to look toward
That of my very own soul
I alone am he, who creates disharmony and imbalance
It is I alone who chooses chaos
Mine wisdom and mine journey
can be of peace and harmony in this life
Yet never through the way of fallible others.

So, might it be

Unto thee do I pray, oh spirit of life.
Oh, wonder of divine essence.
Unto that which contains the elements of; the four directions.
That of the north, keeper of earth.
Of the east, keeper of air.
The south, keeper of fire.
To the west, keeper of water.
Unto all that lives upon and beneath the earth
below and upon the seas
they of the skies and beyond the clouds
far into the many fold stars
tis unto thee, I sing out my open prayer.

Oh thee, that of the unknown
of neither name, nor form, nor gender
that which is the very soul of my being.
It is unto thine presence that I seek
that I may feel thee in my daily breath.
Unto thee, that sends me dreams in sleep.
Tis within this very essence, that true wisdom awaits
to guide me upon the path

Awaken me I cry
for the darkness within. shadows the pure light of thine presence.
Awaken me, that I may live in the pureness of mine own purpose.
May thine will overpower mine follies.
May it be, that I ever be, whole in thine design.
Prepare me for mine ending,
that through thine teachings I be cleared of ignorance.
Allow thine knowledge to penetrate my very being,
as was destined from birth.
May thine hand show the way.
May thine heart beat be as one with mine own.
Allow that mine mind know thine blessings
and my tongue ever speak thine truth.
Avail me of mine duties
that I may live in thine word…….

So, might it be

……..Give unto me direction, that I falter not, against thine wish.
Provide me with worthiness and value,
that neither greed nor envy be mine.
Set me upon thine chartered course
as one, with all of creation.
For this day do I speak with open heart
yet corrupted with emptiness and forlorn ways.

Unto thee of divine essence, I seek to free my spirit soul
from that of human faults and selfish mean……So might it be.

The divide

The divide
Oh, my pride
The shame I create
again, and again
The void in which I live
the falseness of which I give
The deceit I employ
to find a life to enjoy.

Fear,
I know not
another lie.
The point of my being
I know not why

You whoever you are.
lie to me, as I to you.
Why we cry…and onward go,
to kid upon others
to make a show.
Disbelieve and lies so many lips
making endless vocal slips
yet is it just, slight of tongue
or deeper than the lies begun
somewhere so deep inside
separated in that great divide.
The divide of life
one that's pure
the one of which we are so unsure
not we, only me
for you I cannot speak
(only of me that seeks the truth)
so false, so weak, within this great divide
of which I am blind to which I hide
a glimmer comes, a fleeting shadow
sometimes to quick, for me to know.

The essence

That which is the essence of all that is
The seed and wonderment of all life,
Oh, beginning of all things
Oh, name unknown.
I stand before you in search of self.
Thine wisdom do I seek in thine guidance.
For mine journey has become confused.
Through ignorance, greed and separation
The path has become shadowed
Through lack of appreciation of the gift
The gift of life given to share with all
I am caught within the multitude of emotions
created by my own selfish desires.
Laden with mis-information
I walk through shadows
Ever seeking

The Gift

What of you sir, of you, madam, over there?

What choice do you seek?

or has your path also closed the way forward

Forgive me if this choice of speech is incorrect

for it sounds that I doubt your wisdom, that which is, compared to mine.

However, my wisdom is faulty

not structured nor, gospel sound.

My wisdom is more to question, of that which is, my right.

Judge me, judge you, pray why, unless it comes through fear

That both be wrong, and true wisdoms remain hidden

leaving neither you nor I with independent wit.

How be it that we are guilty of; crimes against nature's core?

God forbid this to be so

Though I question each god as man

My payment shall come soon enough.

'Tis then you can gloat with honour.

For, I am as fish. as dog is of bear

I am as the smallest grain, or, greatest of all beasts.

As to the truth, that remains a secret, yet to be unveiled

For this I wait, as each their turn …. The gift, beyond our final door.

The graveyard

A stretch of manmade road, 'twinst buildings, old and new
where nature's greenery stands broken
shadowed with unsightly grey metal towers
rigidly spread across the landscape, ungracefully,
sucking up, life's space and energy.
Criss cross roads each leading to lives unknown
My own thoughts interrupted by, the swish and rumble of speeding cars.

Suddenly the essence of my journey takes a change
There before me stands the open gates of a cemetery, waiting in silence,
A place of past life, yet vibrant, with that of, living bird song
Blooms of color, shades of green, shadowy trees watching over the ever sleeping.
Such truthful silence awaits peacefully within these grounds
Each stone marking a story of life's wonder. Energies of the past and journeys unknown
Slowly I walk between those resting, knowing that, one day, I too shall lay with them,
Maybe a memory, maybe forgotten.
However, one such as I, may stand questioning, this existence of being….
…..From far outside of these hallowed grounds, I hear the echoing of life today
The humdrum of the living, the power race of desperation to conquer time.
Yet here in this stillness, I feel the purity of life, reaching deep within me.
I breathe it in the power of the sun, seeping through my veins,
combining life and death together
How can I portray to you the perfumes of spring? the smoothness of the air
the very essence of life within these grounds.
How can I talk to you of, these who are laid in silence?...................

...........with their wisdom of ages past, of they whose seed has been spread throughout the land.

Of they who shall also come to rest, leaving their legacy's, for that new-born.

Oh, ye of silent grounds, I thank you, for you have shown me,
the value and purpose of time
I have no knowledge of you, and yet, you have shared your quite word
That, I may know life.

I leave now with peace in my heart, as I return into the living world of my time
And though our worlds may be separated,
If truth be unveiled, all share in the presence of life and death
with journeys, yet unknown…..

…. Now here beyond the gates of the sleeping ones, of past life so sadly forgotten
I once again see my world for what it is, I awaken into the reality of the now
the chitter the chatter, The zoom and boom, The walk of life, The recognition.
The time in which I live, the importance of my journey, the importance of all journeys.
The question of; the wonder of each life, the essence of life, this life, which,
we live, share, perceive, as we so wish
yet all leave, when time decides.

The longer sleep

How little I know about you
Your journey compared to mine
I never truly looked into your soul
Whilst we shared this short earth time together
Now though that you are no longer here
I remiss over my selfish ways
For there was much you and I could have shared
Within those awakened days

Now though you sleep that longer sleep
I remain, your presence deep within
Tis only sorrow of lost time I regret

For now, my friend that you have gone
I wonder, was there harmony in your life
Where there answers to all your questions
Were your desires fulfilled, that you left in peace

How little I know, how little we know
About the true wonders and sorrows of another's time
Be it friend, be it parent, sister brother, lover or neighbour
It seems we never know enough

We all share the longer sleep
Yet little appreciate the awakening of birth
How little we know or truly care of another's worth
Here now in silence I offer my heart
that your presence be remembered
for the time we shared this life.

The power of words

The power of words
Created from that of; vision, passion and emotion.
How easily words change life, both for positive and negative
How easily they can be, turned around and altered
Create tears of laughter or tears of woe.
.
They can formulate questions, make statements
They can roll from the tongue or be lifted from;
the very depth of that inner spirit that gives us life
With words we teach, learn, and indoctrinate
We can romance, dream, promote emotions of; love or hate,
create unseen characters that can be friend or foe.

There is no end to the power of word

Word. What is your word?
What would you like to say?
What would you like me to hear?
What is your truth?
Who are you?
Speak to me
with the words of your pure basic self

The search

I am divided of mine own opinion
For is it poetry, or, is it prose
Is it philosophical, or, anti-establishment?
Perhaps it is just the ramblings of someone wishing to express a view.
Whatever, whichever, they are words from the soul,
written through that of, mine own understandings.
With no more than, a desire to create purpose of thought, for the mind of another.
We the human race are very complex and easily waylaid by opinion and emotion
Of our suffering, or presence, there are they who shall seek answers, and there are they who shall not
This of mine personal view has no standing as actual truth,
for I can only surmise from; mine own, actual realities.
Life amazes me. I amaze me
The whole of creation amazes me...
The search for happiness. The desire to have.
The need of acceptance. The jealousy, greed, envy, anger.
The continuous lack of satisfaction.
The willingness to be herded like sheep.
The questionable existence that we have.
The lessons we find so hard to learn.
The thousand questions of; why and how, yet, at the end of the day little has changed.
For, from our earliest histories, prophecies and belief systems,
we remain the same beast.
It is a known truth that there are they who throughout time have had the power to change the rules,
However, it has all been done before. None but repetition
yet never has man had the power to change the elements.
Our species has tried everything from bloodshed to over kindness
And yet, still have not found the satisfactory answer.
Is there one, I believe that there is,
Hard to learn and even harder to share.
For the natural way of things
is but an essence beyond physical knowledge,
a creation that has no given name, nor form.
Remaining purely an essence of; basic originality
I, as many, am far from wise, learning and questioning every day
Tis through this search that I discover deep within
that there is no actual mystery to; the final word of life
It always has been and shall ever remain, simply,
……. the essence of existence.

The secret of purpose

If I could but seek out peace within myself
If I could but find love within myself
If I could but forgive myself
Be my own friend
If I could but share in the wonder of life with passion rather than sorrow
If I could but connect to that which is
If I could but become aware and true to the way of things
If I could but look deep within myself
If I could but find security in my existence
If I could but be at peace with mine own mind
If I could but love me for my existence
If I could but be true.
If I would but allow the essence to govern me
Then the secret of purpose would soon be born within.

The sensation of creation

The sensation of creation
The wonder of imagination
The experience of life's terms
In all that one learns
The Enthrallment of rapture...
In all that we capture
The knowing of growing
The purpose of knowing
The cause and the reason
No matter the season
The moments the feeling
With all we are dealing
The before and thereafter
Is all so revealing
Why hide from the presence
The extreme of the essence
The wonder the wisdom
The universal prism

To become one complete
Never in defeat
To be in true harmony
Accepting synchronicity

To become
The perfect self.

The whisper

The book lays open before me
With its words reaching in to my soul
a wall painting hangs invitingly
offering fantasies to enthrall.

How my heart has longed this pure essence
that offers such creative choice
for within this journey of new-found freedom
I shall hear my Soulmates voice.

No matter how soft the whisper
the spirits shall guide our course
that we together discover our oneness,
which love, and harmony shall endorse.

There is but one way

To speak of my inner desire the passion I love and feel
to pass on to you my truest word, reaching deep into the pureness of your heart
To lift the veil of desire within you, to touch the very essence of your wholeness
I reach out with my very soul, my hand, my heart is yours
walk with me now that you and I may share the eternal dream.

There is but one way, and the way is forward.
There is but one life, that life is now.
There are but two choices, all other is fickle
For, when truth and harmony do not exist
there can only be that of confusions.
as well as delusions.
There is innate and there is inherent, the many contradictions.
There is only one who can decipher, there can only be one of you
The choice lay's open within and before and after
Only one way…. look deeply, and ask yourself,
If there were a path, leading to contentment,
would you take it?
If there was a journey, painless and full of joy,
would you take the first step?
If you discovered, there was another life, deep beyond the shadows
would you desire change?
Should it be that you had an epiphany,
an enlightened moment of your own uniqueness
would you accept it.?
How would it be to simply hear the distant sound of a birds call
catch sight of a budding tree
feel the very essence of all that surrounds you.
the breath of tranquility.
Yet you may ask, where is this great wonder, the pureness that is sought.
'Tis laying deep within your very soul, In the heart, should you dare to peek
It is within and without you at each moment, though shadowed by mortal mind
It is there, a choice, ever awaiting, through awareness and simple being
the path of humankind.
You sleep, you awaken, you rise, the moon has passed, the sun shines forth
the natural world ever in motion moving further on
yet remains in the cycle of things……..

There is but one way

……. Ask of yourself, has yesterday truly passed within your being?
What of old burdens, of fears, desires of the mind.
Freedom is but a choice away, an acceptance.
Yet you remain hidden in shadows of the extinct past
whilst the world turns, and your thoughts speed, ever carried beyond the truth of harmony
Do your actions lead you through desolate times, does your knowledge blind you from faith, from being.
Allow that of natural life embrace you
for only this breath of life shall catty you forward unto the essence of which you are a part.

The Answer is

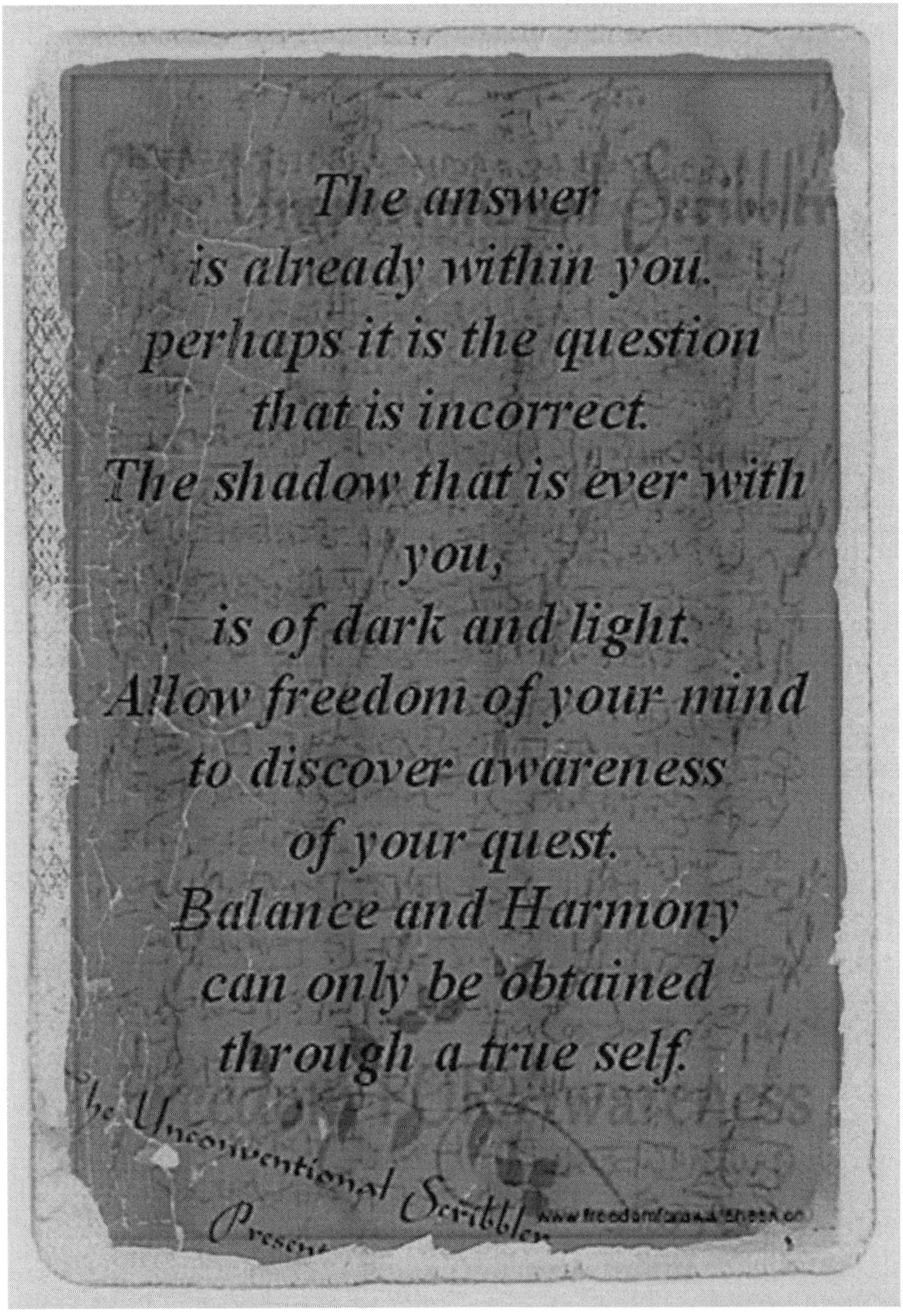

This moment shall pass

What do I expect from myself?
Sitting thoughtless   Not knowing
Do I care?
I suppose I must, or I would not be here
Who or what am I
What is my direction, purpose, value?
Do I have just one true belief?
I am scattered wordless
A shadow of no return
Thankless and selfish
Ignorant of my own conclusions
Do I have a soul, a heart?
Am I invisible to my own presence?
What world is my world?
Dare I speak out?
Or
Must I ever remain in this dark corner of self-pity and loneliness?
Where can I reach to?
What treasure is there that I can hold in my hand, place upon my heart
I am lost, for there are too many pathways to follow
Therefore, I create my own which lead me further into darker corners
I call out to god I hear no conviction in my voice
I am of the devil's blood
Tattered and torn I wander aimlessly
with neither conviction nor structure to this being.
I am unable to communicate even unto myself
I am but a page torn from a book and thrown to the wind
What value can give me peace?
What venture can lead me home?
My being is, my un- being,
For I have little to connect me to the essence of that which is.
A fraud even unto myself
A being in the middle of the ocean,
Refusing to drown,
Yet, floundering daily,
With no land
in sight.

Time moves on

Time moves on

Life moves on

The past remains where it belongs.

Shadows of the day become distant…….

…….as life moves on

Fairy tales of times gone by,

I leave you but with no regret,

for we shared in what was.

and what was,

was washed away with time.

Time my friend or passing foe

shall deal with each in kind

The appreciation of now

is all any of us can have.

Life moves on, as does time

therefore, I move forward into unknown times

and though our paths may cross again,

our journey shall never be the same.

Time of Mind

If I could find the time of mind
Then perhaps I would learn to be a little more kind
Perhaps if I could listen more I would understand more I am sure
Perhaps if I were to look very closely I would see
Direction, correction and many other states of being.
Perhaps if I took time to see all that was happening within, and around me
I would discover peace of mind and perhaps a little harmony
Perhaps if I took the path of truth, I would discover
A pearl of wisdom
The wonder of the unknown,
The loss through desires,
Even the purpose of innocence.
however, patience my friend is sometimes hard to live with
no matter how strong the will to achieve.
To become, to have, to be, to breathe, to understand.

Perhaps the path will become true
Perhaps the essence of life will watch over you
Perhaps this life that is within you will recognize
That as of being, we are as all other forms of life
controlled within the earth and all other boundaries within the universe.

To Find life

And there I found life.
The very pureness of truth, which I believed, had deserted me so long ago,
Yet here it was deep in the heart of my very soul
the essence of me, the very soul of creation.

How I love life,
Yet for all I receive I give little recognition for;
the greatness you bestow all around and within me,
How often I forget to be in gratitude,
remaining ever entangled within mine own delusions.

I should bow before thee in humility,
yet I know that pride and arrogance are ever there.
Is this no more than the folly of a fool who has no true understanding, nor acceptance of; the way toward harmony, that which offers, life beyond earthly wisdoms.

Could that it be different,
Could that the very vision of wisdoms be within mine sight.

Unto thee pure spirit of day and night, creation of all elements,
Tis only through thine essence that I exist, that each simple breath is given.
I implore thee, recognise, see the trauma of mine days.
See how I have been so fooled by the words and actions of fools,
therefore, have I lost mine way.

It is just at that moment when I believe I have found thee in mine sight, my feelings my very being, that I lose thee to the very evils of falseness and destruction.
I can but ask that you lead me beyond this shadowed land of intolerance and foolhardiness in which I live.
Awaken me I pray, for as my life passes by, I discover much cause to regret
Sadly, missing that which is the balance, harmony and choice of true being.
Tis only through thine presence and essence that opens the path; **To find life.**

To name that which is nameless

To name that which is, nameless, to give it form, to make it personal.
How can I talk of that which I know not?
I know of an essence only.
Where within me does it form.
How can I know if it is just another delusion? And, what is delusion
Therefore, unto that which is, that which is the way of all things.
That which is the creation and the destruction, for one cannot be without the other.
Unto that which I blind myself from through ego and indoctrination.
Unto that which for ever speaks within me, yet, I rarely hear.
Unto that which offers me gifts daily which I fail to see, or appreciate
Unto the way, unto the life, unto the truth which lives in all things.
That which is the creation of the natural world, that of original nature
may you forgive and guide me through this, my spiritual ignorance
For I allow myself to become blinded by the choices of others.
There is sameness and there is adaptability, there is oneness and there is variation
there is cause and effect, there is knowing and there is ignorance
yet even knowledge can be an ignorance also, for how can any truly know.
Therefore, I ask only that I awaken unto the essence and become one of harmony
In the way of things, other than mine own ego.

To what point

To what point, that of progress
the ever-tiring mind process
That of seeking out success
discovering the mind in such a mess
With many negatives to access.
endless issues to address
To many wrongs to confess
Never feeling truly blessed
Ever wanting to impress
Desiring that of loves caress
Yet ever caught up in life's distress
Wanting more but getting less
Where lies the truth is but a guess
For the past has been of great duress
And though we long not to transgress
The corrupted mind has no finesse
Leaving us to discover which path is best
To fight the good fight with strength and zest
Or give up hope, and not protest.

Truth within the shadows

The truth is in the shadows; I have searched yet know not where
Many times, have I called out, hearing nought but sad despair
Tis a lonely tale that I tell thee, filled with sorrows and such remorse
Yet I have sought the path of living from each external force.
My woe then is of darkness, where no paradise is to be found
A maze of lost horizons, tis but to hell that I am bound.
Yet, should I once awaken, unto the brightness of the day
Tis a truth the bleak and darkness shall not be far away.
Tis a tale of a fighting soul, of a spirit in lost distress
Where barriers constrain all confessions, even unto death.
In the now, it is with great weariness that I trudge this winding trail
Onward and ever seeking that of wisdom to prevail.
Hear me now or hear me not, what difference can there be.
For I am set to walk in darkness throughout eternity.
However, I end on a cheerful note a word to one and all
No matter the pains of suffering, ever listen for that call
Tis true it may not come this moment, this night, or even the morrow
Yet never give up the search for truth no matter what comes as sorrow.

Tyrannical beast

Having looked for, but never found
Cause of wisdom and common ground.
I submit myself to, the eternal seed.
The gift of wisdom, the purest creed.

I place mine self before natures course
Not that of governance, by human force.

That I have wronged, is not denied
Yet then again, have never tried
to suck the life force from all that lives
as they of power, who never gives
equal opportunity and freedom of mind
to the kindred spirit of humankind.

Tis through grace I find, in my every day
That natural essence shall show the way
And that true hearted souls shall never cease,
The quest of freedom, against the tyrannical beast.

Unto sol

How wonderful each breath I take
For nature knows none other than…that which is.
How wonderful great winds that cleanse
as the sun returns to nurture
How grand the heavens as they open up...
to clear all of negativity and sleep.
Tis time oh wonders we should bow us down
for purification redeems the soul.
May each and sunder from all directions
Give grace unto each other,
for all chaos brings each to roost
creating rebirth and growth of spirit.
Oh hail thee oh winds, oh waters flow
Hail thee deep fire and salt of earth
As you bring forth new light of day
As nature awakens unto thine ways…
…may I also be reborn within.
Hail thee oh chaos,
Hail thee as harmony becomes
For that which is, brings everlasting life
Unto thee oh Sol.... I kneel.

Unto that which is unknown

Unto that which is not known
that which is the essence of all,
is the very seed all elements?
I raise my arms in gratitude
for all that is placed within this realm.
Though it is in sorrow I bow my head
I recognize the ignorance of how I use this life.
Yet still wisdom and serenity do I seek
though in blindness I have travelled.
This misfortune is but mine alone
for I have not followed the golden path.
how many journeys are there to be
before I listen to life's true story.
Daily, sustenance is laid before me,
as is nurture, through natural cause.
What fool could walk away from such grandeur
other than one who hides from truth within shadows.
So, it is unto that which is the very core of life
I lay my heart before you
that my pure originality be restored
as nature, in its ever-created form..

Vanity

Perhaps it is the loneliness
A way of life, that of self-ignorance
A journey with no set direction nor ending,
For the mind chooses another thought
Leading to another path
Where present, past and future become entwined
Creating a world of little knowledge

Perceptions becomes confused
Ever caught in the trap of; the many mindless indoctrinations.

Neither understanding nor Knowing the way of others,
of their need, their want, or desire
There is but a shadowed look in their eyes
I know neither them nor their suffering.
Tis a truth for them only, their journey alone
Not of mine nor mine mind

Though I look vainly into the hearts of many
I recognize that of my own vanity
That of my very own soul
I alone am he, who creates disharmony and imbalance
It is I alone who chooses chaos
Mine wisdom and mine journey can be of peace and harmony
Maybe in this life
Should I come to understand that of empathy and compassion.

What am I doing?

What am I doing? Where am I going? What comes next?
For what purpose, what reason what value?
Whose life is this anyway?
In strength I would walk, were I to be ruthless
Grabbing at every given chance, Yet I remain in weakness
Ever bowing to compassions need
Why, over and over that question rambles
Ever doubting, ever hiding from the reality that surrounds
Why sit back and have nothing? Why care for the woes of others
Do I not have the right to stand up and create a world of joy?
Be gone your pessimistic mind, Come on board you optimistic muse
Let's storm the barriers of solitude make our presence felt.
I welcome selfishness to my bedside
I call out to success in wealth and health
I no longer shall tip toe the floorboards but march on with battering ram force.
Be gone you days of self-pity. Be gone you days of remorse.
No longer your prisoner of sadness. I awaken to a brave new world
Speed forward for time has been wasted. Such poverty of mine have I caused
Yet know there can be no losing, for tis but for the self I shall strive
No longer shall I seek their pleasures nor bow to their whims and woes
For tis now that this life awakens Tis time to smite to grasp and grow.

What is what

What is expected of me, where is my mind,

why are there thoughts floating around with neither rhyme nor reason.

What is reality, what am I doing, what am I meant to do.

Is it true there are rules or is this but fallacy.

Does morality exist? Is there a god? Is there life? is love a false emotion?

I am stuck for words. or am I lost in the meaningless dictionary of all languages.

Why is one person of more worth than another?

Who knows if they who profess to being connected to god, do not just suffer in confusion.

What of all other religions, policies and laws that suit one and not the other.

Who is to say that the law is correct, when it is changeable and so often corrupt?

Who is to say that the church is not the work of evil?

This life is so confusing, full of deceit and illusions.

How can one truth be a truth and another truth be a lie.

Who has the right to demand, who has the right to rebel?

Show me the rule book, not fables written by human hand

Show me the book of rules that comes with birth,

not the indoctrinations of elders who never found pure harmony.

Pathetic, sad the cloud of ignorance, in which humanity live under,

full of misconceptions, delusions and fabricated stories

for the gain of power, of rule, of governance and greed.

So here I share my delusion,

For, do I not have the right to speak of that which I know not

……….. as any other upon this earth...

Words of Wisdom

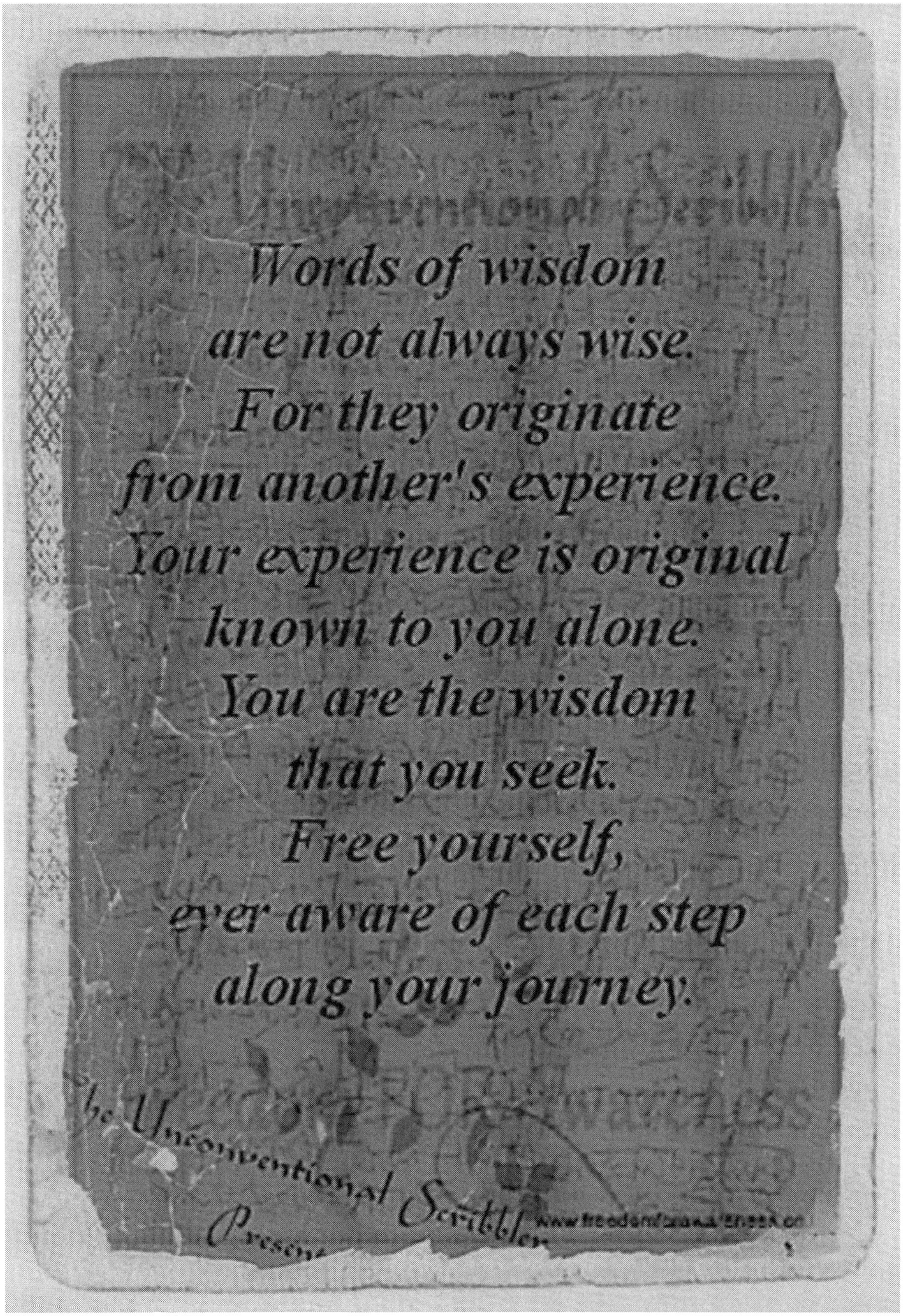

Who rules

What do we really know of self
Of its mission
What do we know of God and his purpose?
What of the spirit, the soul, that of life's intention.
What knowledge of that which is actual.

God in any language means other than,
taking away responsibility for one's actions
In the name of God, millions of innocents have been slaughtered,
Lands pillaged
Crimes of life committed
What is human other than, an it.
It is no more, nor less than any other

I look within this self
See it for what it is and what it does
This does not bring me happiness
For when I compare it to the natural world
of others that may surrounds me
I see, greed, want and destruction.
The emotions, the cravings, the dissatisfaction,
The loss, and, the confusion.

Do not agree with me nor dis-agree
Look to your own self
Hear your own mental discussions
Feel what is real for your being
Discover the sense of purpose and action
Check out the thought process
How far can you trust your imaginations?
How can you discern one thought process from another?
Which is correct which is not
Decisions based on what wisdom
Who's instruction?
Appropriate behaviour, according to?

Life is divided into two
That which is called good and that known as bad…. Two opposites
Day night, right wrong, beautiful, ugly
Each presence upon this earth having two sides at any given time
that match, or, contradict, circumstances of the moment
However, who are we to judge which is correct, **and by who's rule.**

Wisdoms word

I am not he of the shadows'
Nor he of the light, nor that of earth, nor sea, nor sky.
I am no more than a seeker, within a time of mindlessness.

'Tis this which is mine truth, for awakening comes not easily.
Yet at the same time, I am an untruth, in many manners and, thoughtless thoughts.
It is I who continues to alter facts, to prove mine own identity above all else.
How is it, that I know not, mine own path and balance.
Why is it that I cannot revel in the arms of harmony?
Where can I find this mental gateway to freedom?
how do I escape that which leads me only further into darkness?
I seek but just a little light with which to find my way.
That I may know that of; purpose and actuality.
Alas I falter, with mine world and Identity,
for it is as though, there is no blessing for my given path.
For that which connects to that of purest thought,
was early robbed from childhood heart.
Perhaps this the why of mine fear, of mine emptiness.
Should it be, that my ego be reduced to tears, what then for; this mis-happened being.
Deafened to the voice of truth that whispers softly of wisdoms and love.
Awaken fool, \I chide mine self,
for each second spent in ignorance misses that of life's joy.

'Tis then only that of; pride and arrogance, remains within the soul.
I stand surrounded by memories path,
I seek blessings of, that which is, yet can bow down only in lack of spirit.
I ask only that I find mine natural course, that I live within the realm of light.
I await, I long for, I listen out for that of wisdoms word to engulf me

You are loved

You are loved
Who are you?
What does it matter?
You exist
I am glad that you exist...
Your form, culture, gender is of little importance to me,
We breathe the same air
How amazing you and I are
What we do, what we see, what we perceive
I can feel your presence at this moment, we may never meet,
Yet we are sharing an existence in time.

What at this moment is happening within your sphere of existence?
The combinations of actuality are far too many to conceive.

All of this is way beyond my intelligence or knowledge as way beyond yours.
Yet I feel that I now you
That pain that you suffer
That laughter that surrounds you
Those questions that you ask
Those doubts that you have
That pleasure that you seek.
There is so much that you could teach me, for your wisdom is unique unto you
Our experiences are life,, yet I cannot live yours, as you cannot live mine
However, we can both share empathy.

Here we are a connection within an existence
valid for one as another.
Who are you?
What is the very essence of you?
Not that which has become taught or indoctrinated
But that which is so deep within you
You can feel it, that natural originality
We will never share this for there are not the words to express
Yet we are as one, a species amid the many of creation
What is this creation?
What is this seed of life you and I share?
Who do you call on for wisdom?
What life wells up within you when you stand outside of the complications of mind?
Whoever you are, you are purpose, you are reason, and you are cause and effect
You are the thousand and one reasons that I am also alive
You are my life as I am yours………

You are loved

……. How, can I not love you?

Though I may act guarded and insecure
Though I may be very protective of my own being
That spark lies deep within me
What part of me, I do not know
I cannot fathom the essence of me that makes me a purpose,
And you my friend cannot tell me, nor I you
Yet we will pass through the lives of many others
who are also the answer to the essence of time.
Journey well my friend for we may pass each other as friend or foe
However we know that we are connected by the miracle of original being.
Therefore I love you, Beyond your being, for I reach into the very depth of your soul.

Finale

A note to myself.

Hope care and happiness
A desire to discover, the light of wisdom within.
Purpose value and worthiness,
The element that is, individual truth.
Seeking the freedom for; awareness.
Awareness of the self and all it means,
Stripping that self of; dogma and Indoctrination.
In effect becoming and understanding, the very core of actual being.
The search for love and fulfilment,
reduced through that other than that which is your true essence.
Step back for just one moment, allow your whole being to be still,
'tis is within your own space you can see the clouding of your thoughts.
Breathe in heavens soul, allow that which has, neither name, form, nor, gender
Enter your being, with neither, judgement, nor, expectation.
Harken unto the inner voice.
Do not fear should you feel physical emptiness, for it is within this emptiness
that truth vibrates from the very nature of; that which is.
Release yourself into the void, far from the words of others,
for it is they who have created, the confusion and loss of your pure ipseity.

Though your life may have been filled with many misgivings, they can only belong in a past that has no rightful place in the present moment. Allow not the emotions of the past to blind you from nature's own.
Be free, without fear, nor, fear of loss, for the material world abounds in many distortions as does the unpredictable mind.
Allow nature's grace to guide you, allow yourself to drift into, her nurturing arms.
Allow yourself to, taste, feel, hear, smell and visualize that which is pure in all way's, giving light where there is darkness.
Remove yourself from, tales and fables passed on by the many, for only one individual can truly live and learn from their own story.
Balance yourself in harmony and gratitude for your living being, created through purposes unknown.
Speak not of any other, nor think of their failings or success, for each second is precious unto you.
The way is within you, as is, in each. There is no rule to the pureness of life,
other than that, which, is designed for existence throughout the universe.

For hope, for care, for happiness.
Seek no longer through the voices of mankind.
Simply allow the unknown to enter and give guidance,
This is your path to a contented existence...

These following empty pages belong to you

I wonder if you were to write from your deepest self, what you may find

Fear not Creativity...for you are of the created nature that surrounds.

Scribble, Scrawl, Doodle, sketch, fear not my friend to over stretch.

So, we come to the last pages of, empty white space
Of discovering the freedom of scribble and grace.
However, should you choose to turn back to page one.
There are plenty of spaces to write and have fun.

May Harmony Balance and Well-being

Ever bring you Contentment in all you do.

The Unconventional Scribbler 2018

31628952R00101

Printed in Poland
by Amazon Fulfillment
Poland Sp. z o.o., Wrocław